Conexus de Caseus

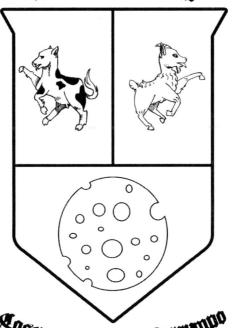

Caseus Nunquam Corrumpo

The Secrets of the Cheese Syndicate

FOR YOUR EYES ONLY

Cheese Syndicate Property

Happy Birthday!

Donna St. Cyr

Children's Brains are Yummy Books
Austin, Texas

The Secrets of the Cheese Syndicate

Text Copyright © 2009 by Donna St. Cyr

Cover Images:
Boy's Photo © Stockbyte Royalty Free Photograph/Getty Images
Cheese Image © Fotosearch
Paperclip Image © Fotosearch

For more information, write:
CBAY Books
PO Box 92411
Austin, TX 78709

First Edition 2009
ISBN(10): 1-933767-10-3
ISBN (13): 978-1-933767-10-9
CIP data available.

Children's Brains are Yummy Books
Austin, Texas
www.cbaybooks.com

Printed in the United States by United Graphics Inc.
For more production information, please go to
www.cbaybooks.com/resources/cpsia.html

For Dad, with love.

INTER-OFFICE MEMORANDUM

To: Entire Cheese Syndicate Staff
From: Madame Gorgonzola

Attention Friends of Cheese:

Within this file you will find field notes from our newest member's first assigned mission.

I encourage each of you to read the file carefully. Our agent showed excellent command of our secret practices and devised some new methods to achieve his goal. Perhaps even the ancients could learn a new trick from his ingenuity, no?

As always, commit these details to memory and burn this file after reading. There will be no way to access this information at a later date. The world must continue to keep its blissful ignorance of our organization.

File Contents:

1/Today's Top Ten/1

2/The Effervescent Elixir Company/11

3/Meeting Madame Gorgonzola/19

4/Syndicate Secrets/30

5/Somewhere in the Darkness/42

6/On the Beach/53

7/Into Neptune's Realm/64

8/Journey to the Crater/73

9/Into the Bowels of the Earth/88

10/The Lost City/104

11/The Gorgon Takes the Cheese/111

12/The Poseidon Adventure/120

13/Mazes and Manticores/131

14/Into the Labyrinth/139

15/Janine Saves the Day/150

Chapter 1

Today's Top Ten

Hello, my name is Robert, and I have a problem. Actually, today I had lots of problems. I usually make a "Top Ten" list, but today I had to throw in a couple of bonus ones.

I woke up this morning, and it was raining. This created two problems. First, Mom made me wear my geeky galoshes over my shoes. Second, we had inside recess—no basketball. Problem number three was Janine, my ten-year-old little sister. She's usually my number one problem. She follows me everywhere and butts in on all my conversations with my friends.

This morning, my friend Mel dropped her pencil bag on the bus. When I picked it up and gave it back to her, Janine popped over the seat behind me singing, "Robert and Melanie sitting in a tree, K-I-S-S-I-N-G." I gave her my "I'm going to kill you when we get home" look and she shut up, but not before she made disgusting lip smackers loud enough for the entire bus to hear. There have been

1

times I've wished I was an only child. Today was one of those times.

My problem list rounded out by forgetting to do my math homework, getting stuck-up Constance Snodgrass for my science partner, eating veggie burgers for lunch, receiving a lecture from Mrs. Peterson about passing notes, and finally, getting a ponytail slap from Janine in the afternoon bus line because I refused to carry her backpack home. It's pink and weighs a ton. I think she carries everything she owns in it. While Janine pitched a royal fit, Coach Hawkins walked by.

"Robert," he said, "why don't you be a gentleman and help out your little sister?" If it had been anyone but Coach, I'd have had a million excuses, but basketball tryouts for the 6th grade team were coming up, so instead I just swallowed hard.

"Yes sir, Coach," I said. "I was just going to do that." I gave Janine a shove after Coach turned away, picked up her stinky old backpack, and carried it to the bus. That brought my list up to eight things that had already gone wrong today.

I dumped Janine's backpack into the first seat and high-tailed it to the back of the bus. I slouched low so she wouldn't follow me. As the bus rumbled out of the parking lot, I heard the *clink clink* of something rolling toward my seat. It's amazing the kind of junk that litters the back of a bus. I reached down and scooped up a green glass bottle right before it hit my foot. When I shook it up, the bottle glowed like a fireworks display. I turned it over and read the label:

> *Madame Gorgonzola's Effervescent Elixir!*
> *Good for what ails you: Reduces severe headache pain, debilitating toothache pain, agonizing back pain, cramping leg pain and irritating little sister pain.*

I certainly had a big headache. I opened the bottle, releasing a soothing peppermint smell, and rubbed some on my forehead, just like the directions said. Closing my eyes, I leaned back in my seat, thinking this had been the best moment of my day. Something tugged on my arm. Without warning, my headache got worse.

"Whatchya got there, Robert?" Janine's shrill voice pierced my eardrums. "Give me some!" she demanded.

Before I could stop her, Janine yanked the bottle from my hand and, like a thirsty camel, guzzled down all of Madame Gorgonzola's Effervescent Elixir.

"Hey!" I wrestled the bottle back from her grimy little hands. "Are you crazy? You don't know what's in there! Besides, hasn't anyone ever told you not to grab?"

"That's pretty good," Janine continued, oblivious to my reprimand, "got any more?"

"No! Beat it!" I must've looked furious, because the smile faded from her face, and Janine scooted back to her seat at the front of the bus without another word. I looked at the bottle. It seemed harmless, but it would serve her right if she got a horrible stomachache. Stuffing it into my backpack, I laid my head against the seat again. Instantly, I was whiplashed into the seat in front of me as the driver slammed on the brakes. We were home.

"Move it, sister." I scowled at Janine, who blocked the bus doorway.

She shook her head violently and pointed to Mademoiselle Bella, the neighbor's hyperactive Labrador who was loose out front, racing around in circles.

"Robert, Bella's going to attack me," Janine said. Her eyes were wide, and she was shaking.

Bella wasn't a bad dog, really. But Janine had so many key chains dangling from her stupid backpack that Bella took it as a personal invitation to play fetch. She usually knocked Janine down trying to retrieve one of the mini-balls hanging from the zipper pull. Janine wasn't afraid of much, but she hated it when Bella took a bite out of her backpack.

Although I didn't sympathize with her, I really wanted out of the bus, so I scooped up the wretched bag and carried it up the walk. Bella made a beeline for me as soon as she saw the bangles flash. Janine raced ahead and made it through the front door unscathed. Bella managed to grab one string of beads before I pulled the bag through the front door.

"Robert!" Janine yelled when she saw the damage. "I'm telling Mom."

"Mom, we're home!" I yelled. I scowled at Janine, dropped her precious cargo on the hall rug, and headed straight to the sanctuary of my room. Two hours later, I still lay on my bed with my headphones on. When I cranked the volume up loud, they drowned out the sounds of family life. Suddenly, the sound went dead. I looked up. My frowning mom twirled the headphone cord she'd just unplugged.

"Robert, I've been calling you for five minutes!" She dropped the wire, put her hands on her hips, and glared at me. I stared back at her for a second until she threw up her hands and said, "Dinner's ready."

"Sorry, Mom. I didn't hear you," I said, but she had

already left the room. I hurried down the hall and into the kitchen. Janine smirked at me as I took my seat.

"Robert, how many times do I have to tell you?" Mom wasn't expecting an answer. She was lecturing. "Dinner is at 6:00. Try to make an effort to get into the kitchen so I don't have to call Search and Rescue to find you."

"Sorry, Mom." I tried to sound apologetic. She wasn't so bad, just stressed. Anyone who had to put up with Janine would be stressed. Combine that with the fact that my dad had split two years back, and she's had it tough. I try not to give her too much grief, but she'd gone overboard with this "The Family Will Have Dinner Together Every Night" program. I know she got it from the single parenting class at the community center because she never used to worry about dinner. I think she doesn't want us to be all screwed up just because Dad skipped out.

Dinner was the usual quick fix chicken and potatoes, something green, and some fruit. Mom isn't a gourmet cook, but she tries to be balanced.

"Janine, don't slouch," Mom nagged.

"I'm not slouching," Janine said, but Mom had already moved on to other things.

"Robert, I have to work an extra shift at the hospital tonight, so you'll have to watch Janine," she said.

"Yeah, whatever," I mumbled pushing the green stuff around on my plate. What was it anyway? Green beans? Peas? Creamed spinach? Janine proceeded to drone on about every insignificant detail of her day. My head had started to droop into the mashed potatoes when Mom's voice roused me.

"Okay, sweeties, Mrs. Mumphrey is home next door if you need anything. I've got to run." She gave us both a peck on the head and was out the door.

"Looks like it's just you and me, Robert." Janine smiled sweetly. "Are you going to play chess with me?"

"Not a chance." Janine was a demon at chess. I could never figure out how she'd gotten to be so good, but she could beat me every time I played her. I looked up from my almost empty plate. "And quit slouching!"

"*I am not slouching*!" Janine leaned over the table to yell back at me.

"Then you must be shrinking." I laughed. Shrinking? I choked on my last gulp of milk, and it sputtered through my nose.

"Eww, Robert!" Janine shrieked. "Milk snot! Disgusting!"

I peered at her from across the table.

Her nose barely cleared the edge of her plate. She was definitely shorter than yesterday.

"Stop staring at me, Robert," Janine said, putting her hands on her hips. "You're giving me the creeps!" She shuddered as if she had a chill.

She couldn't possibly be shrinking. I rubbed my eyes and stared at her some more. Goosebumps started to form on my own arms and the hair began to stand on end. Why was Janine shrinking? It didn't make any sense. Must be some type of optical illusion.

"Earth to Robert," Janine said. She tapped my head with her finger.

"What?" I said as I swatted her hand away. She was as irritating as a gnat.

"Where'd you get that fizzy stuff you had on the bus today? It was a million times better than those no-name sodas Mom always buys. What'd you say it was called?"

"Madame Gor…" I stopped in midsentence. "Never mind what it was called. I don't have any more." I stared at her again. Could this have anything to do with that stuff in the bottle? "No way."

"No way, what?"

"What?" I looked at Janine. Why wouldn't she leave me alone? I needed to think.

"You just said, 'no way,'" Janine answered.

"Did not," I said.

8

"Did too."

"Whatever," I said.

"So, no way, what?" Janine asked, stomping her foot.

"No way I'm going to ever get my homework done because I got in trouble with Mrs. Peterson today and —"

Janine cut me off. "Oh, you've got punish work. I'm telling Mom."

I let her think she was right. After all, I did get into trouble for passing notes. A little negotiation here would give me the time I needed to find out if I was crazy or Janine was really shrinking. I had to go find that bottle. "Look, Janine. It's going to take me all night to do this. Would you please not tell Mom?"

"What's in it for me?

"I'll let you borrow my MP3 player."

"How long can I have it?" She leaned forward in her negotiating stance.

"You can have it until tomorrow morning, but you have to clean up the kitchen too."

Janine thought about it for a little while. "Okay, deal. But you have to do my bathroom duty tomorrow, and I'm not cleaning up that!" She snorted and pointed to the milk mucous I'd left all over the table.

"Okay," I said. It was gross after all, bubbly and white,

oozing across the plastic placemat. I carefully surrounded it with a bunch of napkins so I wouldn't have to touch it.

"You know," Janine gloated over me while she picked up the plates, "when Mom finds out about this, you'll probably get into trouble all over again."

I watched her load the dishwasher. Using my thumb and forefinger, I tried to measure her from my seat. She was definitely smaller than this morning, and I had no rational explanation for it. This was turning into a major problem.

"Probably," I whispered.

Chapter 2

The Effervescent Elixir Company

I hurried into my room and dug my backpack out. I unzipped it and rifled through the contents. Yesterday's lunch, not too moldy yet. Science test, C-. Social studies book, can't forget to do my homework again. Permission slip for basketball tryouts, very important. Where was that bottle? Finally, I dumped everything out onto the floor. The bottle landed on top of the pile and rolled under the bed.

I got down on my stomach and stuck my arm in as far as it would go. The bottle's cap was at the tips of my fingers, but I couldn't get hold of it. It seemed to want to stay hidden under the bed. An old boot was lying under a pile of bubble gum wrappers, so I grabbed it and gave the bottle a push. It emerged from the bed, rolling for the closet. I wrapped my fingers around it before it entered that black hole.

I bounced down on my unmade bed and examined the bottle more closely. Beneath the Effervescent Elixir label was a whole paragraph written in very small print. Tiny, minute print. I couldn't even read it. I needed a magnifying glass, so I snuck into Mom's bedroom and swiped her reading glasses. Back in my sanctuary, I felt foolish squinting through her spectacles, but at least no one could see me. The paragraph said:

> *The person in possession of this bottle assumes all responsibility for the use of its contents. The Effervescent Elixir Company cannot be held liable for any mishaps occurring from the failure to read and follow all instructions exactly. If you are reading this information, the Effervescent Elixir Company assumes you have failed to use our product in the intended manner. The Effervescent Elixir Company continues to assume no responsibility for your stupidity. However, it is imperative you call our Consumer Safety Hotline immediately. Call 243-373-4357 (CHEESE-HELP). Why are you still reading this? Pick up the phone and call us now! You are wasting precious time!*

The fine print continued, but I didn't read any more. I jumped up to get the phone, tripped over my backpack pile, and bruised my knee. Kicking the straps off my feet, I hobbled over to my phone and punched in the numbers. This was crazy! It couldn't even be a real phone number. But it was ringing.

"Hello. Welcome to the Effervescent Elixir Consumer Safety Hotline," a cheery voice answered. "This is Brie speaking. How may I help you?"

"Hi, my sister drank some of your elixir and . . ."

She cut me off in mid-sentence. "Which elixir did she ingest, sir?" she asked in that sweet voice teachers use when they think you're an idiot.

"Madame Gorgonzola's . . ."

She cut me off again. "I'm sorry sir. You will have to speak to someone in the Reductions Department. May I put you on hold?"

Without waiting for an answer, she plugged me into that awful "Wait on the Phone" music. The only thing was, I couldn't understand anything. The lyrics were in another language. How'd I get into this situation anyway? How could Janine be shrinking? Why was I talking to people with names like cheeses? What had I done to deserve any of this?

"Mr. Havarti speaking," a smooth voice interrupted the music. "Would you please state your problem?"

"My sister drank a bottle of your elixir."

"Which elixir, sir?" he asked with a sigh.

"How many do you have?"

"Twenty-three in all. But we are retiring Madame Asiago's at the end of the year."

"It was Madame Gorgonzola's."

"A whole bottle of Madame Gorgonzola's?" He coughed through the phone.

"Yeah, pretty much the whole bottle. I tried to stop her but—"

"Excuse me, but I need to refer you to our 'Major Problem' department. I am not authorized to handle your situation. Please hold." I was stuck with the music again. This was ridiculous. Janine was ruining my night. If she wasn't such a pest to begin with, I wouldn't be wasting my time on hold with this crazy company.

"Hello. Thank you for holding. This is Mrs. Reggianito. How may I help you?" I could tell by her no-nonsense tone that this lady had some power. Maybe I'd finally get somewhere with her.

"I've tried to explain this twice already," I shouted into the phone. "Janine drank your elixir and now she's shrinking!"

14

"There's no need to get upset Mr. . . What did you say your name was?" she asked, none too politely.

"Robert."

"Mr. Robert, I need a few more pieces of information, and we'll have you fixed up in a jiffy. Of course, the Effervescent Elixir Company solves these problems as a customer courtesy. We are in no way claiming responsibility for your misuse of our product."

"I didn't misuse your product. Janine did!"

"How old is Janine, Mr. Robert?"

"Ten."

"If you read Section II, Paragraph IV of our disclaimer, you will notice that any sisters under the age of twelve are not liable for their actions. Our company holds you responsible for all reckless acts committed by your little sister."

"Figures," I moaned.

"Now, at what time did Janine drink the elixir?"

"On the bus this afternoon, about 3:30, I think."

"Accuracy is important if we are going to help you, Mr. Robert."

"Then 3:35." I made that up. I didn't see how the exact time she drank the stuff had anything to do with fixing our problem.

"Good. How much did she ingest?"

"The whole bottle, I already told the other guy that." How many times was I going to have to repeat the same story?

"Yes, I understand. But was the bottle completely full?" she asked.

"Yeah."

"Oh, that changes things. Are you sure it had not been opened before she drank it?" She grilled me as if she was a police detective. I didn't see how this was going to help the situation at all.

"Well, I had rubbed some on my temples." I remembered that had been the best moment of my miserable day.

"Thank you for that little detail, Mr. Robert. Without it, I would have needed to transfer you to our 'Hopeless Cases' department." She paused. "As it is, I think I can help you. However, this is a very serious case of Elixir Abuse. I must warn you that reversing the effects of the elixir will not be easy. Are you prepared to do what is necessary to return Janine to her proper stature, Mr. Robert?"

"Yeah, I think so. Look, we have to get this done before Mom gets home. She'll be back in eight hours."

"You are correct, Mr. Robert. Time is of the essence. I have set up an appointment for you with Madame

Gorgonzola at 8:13 p.m. Please do not be late. Goodbye, and thank you for calling the Effervescent Elixir Company."

She hung up.

This Mrs. Reggi-whoever was out of her mind. I couldn't leave the house at 8:13. I was babysitting. 8:13? That was in three minutes. Mom wasn't going to like it, but Janine would have to fend for herself. She was perfectly capable. I probably was going to get into trouble, but there was no way I was taking Janine with me.

I had no idea where the Effervescent Elixir Company was. I looked at the clock—8:12. She said not to be late. I picked up the bottle and searched the label for an address. Blazing letters appeared through the glass. They said:

Look inside.

I raised the bottle to the light and brought it close to my eye. It looked like a green kaleidoscope, and it felt like a wind tunnel. This was definitely not normal. The sound of rushing air was so loud I felt like I'd somehow gotten between two freight trains. My heart pounded as I tried to wrap my feet around the chair legs, but before I could latch onto anything, the vortex sucked me in, headfirst. I felt like icing squeezing through one of those cake decorator tips.

I tumbled to a halt in front of a tall, green glass building. It was surrounded by other skyscrapers, all made of the same weird shade of glass. The wind stopped, and I felt my head, arms, and legs to make sure I'd made it through in one piece. Everything seemed okay, and I took a deep breath. I looked at my watch—8:13. I needed to hurry, so I raced up the steps and burst through the doors marked:

Effervescent Elixir Company
M. Gorgonzola, C.E.O.

Chapter 3

Meeting Madame Gorgonzola

It was eerily quiet inside the cool, dimly lit building. No one was around, so I walked across the cavernous lobby toward the only door I saw, about 100 feet away. A tiny sliver of light escaped through the crack at the bottom. My footsteps echoed across the marble floor, breaking the stillness. It creeped me out.

When I reached the threshold, the door swung open silently, as if on cue. A wave of odor pushed out of the doorway, crashing over me and literally knocking me off my feet. My butt hit the marble floor. It was awfully hard. Man, what was that smell? I wasn't sure I wanted to meet whatever was inside that office.

"Come in," a gravelly voice commanded. I got up and walked hesitantly into the room. Behind the desk sat a woman, if you could call her that. I assumed it was Madame Gorgonzola.

The stink seemed to emanate from her desk. She was huge, with voluminous arms that looked like they might crumble apart any minute. Her head looked like a cheese wheel with beady eyes sunken deep near the center. Her face, all of her skin, in fact, was a pale creamy color streaked with blue-green veins. She was ugly. She smelled bad. I wanted to get out of there.

"So good of you to come, Robert," the cheese head spoke. "Please have a seat." She gestured toward a chair at the side of her desk.

"Uh, no thanks. I think I'll stand." I wanted to be ready for a quick getaway.

"You need my help, no?" she nodded, bouncing her head.

"Yeah. You see my sister . . ."

She motioned for silence. "I am well aware of your situation, Robert. I am sorry to say, though, that you do not seem to be suitable material for our company."

"Suitable material? Look, I don't know what you're talking about. I just need to get my sister blown up," I blurted out. I shook my head, realizing that hadn't come out quite right. "Wait, I don't mean blown up. I mean un-shrunk."

"'Tis a pity." Her head bobbled as she stared down at her desk.

"What's a pity?"

"We held out such hope for you." She gazed back at me.

"Hope? For me?" I felt my voice rising higher and higher. "What are you talking about? It's my sister who needs you." I'd had about enough of Madame Stinky Cheese's runaround. And her stench was going to make me puke.

"I see I must speak plainly to you, no?"

"Yes!"

"Robert, you did not find that bottle of my elixir. It found you. You might have been our next agent."

"Agent? What kind of agent? And who is we?" I waved my hand back and forth in front of my nose, trying to get a breath of fresh air. "And could you open a window or something? I don't mean to be rude, but the smell in here is about to kill me."

"We are the Secret Syndicate of Cheese," she said as she stared off into space. "We have existed from time immemorial. Our brotherhood defends all corners of the world from evil and bad taste." After she paused a moment, she looked back at me. "Robert, I apologize for the odor. I am quite old and have grown stronger than humans can stand, I am afraid." Reaching toward me, she picked up a small round tin. "Eat this cracker, and you shall be able to tolerate the smell." She opened the tin and offered me the cracker. "Take it, no?"

Against my better judgment, I took the cracker. I was already her hostage in this office, not to mention inside the bottle. I took a tiny bite. The smell lessened slightly. I ate the whole thing. Ah! I could breathe again. What was that she said about a secret agent? She must have the wrong guy.

"Why me?" I could look at her now that the smell was gone.

"You know your name, no?"

"Of course, I'm Robert Montasio." How stupid did she think I was?

"Does that mean nothing to you?" She stared at me.

"Should it?" I cocked my head sideways.

"Aye, yigh, yigh!" She slapped her head in frustration, sprinkling cheese crumbs everywhere. "Do they teach you nothing today?" Madame Gorgonzola shook her head back and forth slowly.

I stared dumbly at her. She was more than a little wacko.

"You, boy, are the penultimate descendant of a great family of cheese makers. From the Mountain Montasio you come. You have the power to join the Syndicate. This is why the bottle found you. You understand this, no?"

"No. I don't understand. Nobody in my family makes cheese. My mom's a nurse. My dad's a . . . well, he used to run a restaurant," I finished in a whisper.

"And he does this no longer?" She questioned me.

"I haven't spoken to him in two years." I didn't want to think about my dad. "I don't know where he lives." I collapsed into the chair.

"Mama mia!" She threw up her hands. "Do you know nothing about his secret life?"

"Secret life?" This was getting too weird.

"Marco Montasio was my best agent. His communications ceased approximately two years past while on an undercover mission to retrieve the missing Mystic Cheese of Eliki, which has been lost for over three thousand years."

"But I— " I opened my mouth to protest, but couldn't bring myself to say it. All this time I thought he was living it up on the French Riviera. He had been at a wine auction there when he deserted us. My jaw dropped.

"I know what you are thinking. Marco Montasio is not the 'running off' kind, no?"

I thought about my father for the first time in a long while. I was very angry when he left. I loved him so much—and I thought he loved us.

One day Mom sat Janine and me down and just said plainly, "Your father isn't coming back, and I don't want to talk about it." After that, she was totally silent about the whole thing. I never brought it up because I thought it would hurt her feelings. Well, that's not entirely true. I didn't want to talk about it either. I couldn't understand how he had done that to us. It didn't make any sense at all. And it hurt to think about. As time passed, and we didn't hear from him, I assumed he had forgotten us.

In fact, I had assumed he'd run off with some woman. So I sealed him into a dusty corner of my mind. Maybe I was wrong. I looked at Madame Gorgonzola. "No, he wasn't the running off kind." I shuffled my feet and stared back down at my grungy sneakers.

"Trust your instincts, then." Her head wobbled toward me. "You were chosen to complete his mission. You are very young yet." She paused a moment. "I probably should have given you more years before calling you into service, but times are desperate, and I did not have many options." She sat tapping her desk. It looked like she was trying to make a decision. She looked up at me again. "Perhaps you can still succeed."

I thought about my dad. According to this lady, he

hadn't really deserted us after all. This was so crazy. But if he was in trouble I had to do something. I had to finish his mission. I looked into Madame Gorgonzola's eyes. "I know I can do it," I whispered.

"Robert, you just might," she said. I think she tried to smile because little bits of cheese crumbled down from her cheeks, making a pile on her desk.

"But what about Janine?" I asked, remembering why I'd come here in the first place.

"Ah, yes. Little Janine. She can be quite annoying, no?"

"Yes!" Finally, someone who understood what it was like to put up with Janine.

"She will have to go with you on the journey," Madame Gorgonzola said with authority.

"What? No way!" I wailed.

"As you failed in your duties to safeguard the elixir, you have no choice but to bring her along. Until she is cured, she is your responsibility." I could tell there was no negotiation on this point. She continued, "Do not worry, young Robert. If you find the Mystic Cheese of Eliki, it has the power to restore Janine to her former self. This is good, no?"

"No. I mean, yes. I think so." I was so confused I couldn't even give a straight answer.

"Good. Then it is settled. If the membership will have you, you shall become a neophyte of the Secret Cheese Syndicate. Prepare to take the oath."

I got up slowly. "Wait. Madame Gorgonzola?" I said softly.

She looked up at me. "You are having second thoughts, no?"

"No. No second thoughts. But is there a chance I could find my father while I'm looking for this Eliki cheese?" I asked, daring to hope she'd say "yes."

"There is always a chance, young Robert." She rose and walked around her desk to pat me on the shoulder, but the tips of her fingers crumbled against my shirt. She withdrew her hand and shook her head. "I am a very old cheese," she said sadly.

Madame Gorgonzola shuffled toward the door. "Follow me, Robert. The installation ceremony is about to begin."

As I followed her back into the lobby of the building, I noticed it was no longer empty. Many people stood there in a semicircle. I don't know how they all got there. Some were short and round. Some were streaked, like Madame Gorgonzola. Bright red, waxy clothing covered some. Others wore rough looking burlap. They whispered to each other as we approached. It was strange, but some of them seemed very familiar. Like maybe I'd seen them at the wine and cheese tastings my Dad used to have at his restaurant. I wondered if any of them had been there before.

"Friends of Cheese," Madame Gorgonzola's voice rose through the hall. The conversations died away, and everyone turned their attention to her.

"I now present Robert Montasio for your approval. He wishes to join the Syndicate. What say you?"

"He is too young," a fat greasy voice objected.

I am not! I thought, looking for the speaker. She sounded mean.

"He is too careless," a smooth, creamy voice murmured. I couldn't see this voice either, but it sounded like my old math teacher who always said I didn't pay enough attention.

My eyes sank to the floor as I listened to the others call out their complaints. What if they didn't approve?

"He had no knowledge. He must be given a chance to prove himself," a rough voice spoke in my defense.

Finally. Someone who didn't think I was a total screw-up. I looked through the crowd to see a tall thin fellow with weather-beaten and very dry skin. I was grateful that not everyone was against me.

"Give him a chance," other voices joined the debate. It seemed like the opinions started to flow in my favor.

"The time to vote has come," Madame Gorgonzola finally called out. "All in favor of allowing Robert Montasio into the Syndicate, say 'Aye.'"

A chorus of "Ayes" rose up.

"All opposed." There was a long silence. Wow! After all those first objections, I thought for sure someone would vote against me. Maybe they liked to be unanimous.

"It is settled then." Madame Gorgonzola motioned to me. "Robert Montasio, please step forward."

I walked up to her. She lightly placed her hands on my shoulders. This time her fingertips did not disintegrate.

"Robert Montasio, do you solemnly swear to uphold the principles of the Secret Cheese Syndicate, promising never to reveal its secrets and working to use its powers to improve the lives and good taste of everyone you meet?"

"Uh, yes," I said, not sure what I had just promised.

"Then by the power vested in me by the Syndicate, I pronounce you Neophyte of the Order of the Cheese. Congratulations."

I looked up to see the crowd disperse in twos and threes. They wandered across the hall and disappeared into a mist. Soon I was left alone in the hall with Madame Gorgonzola.

"Just one more thing," I said, still trying to understand everything. "You said I was the penultimate descendent of the Montasio family. What's a penultimate?"

"You are next to last."

"Who's the last descendant?"

"Why, Janine, of course. Now come. There is much work to do, no?"

Chapter 4

Syndicate Secrets

I followed Madame Gorgonzola back to her office. She shuffled toward a bookshelf behind her desk, leaning slightly to the right as she walked, almost as if she was about to fall over.

"Aha. Here it is," she said, as her fingers located the correct volume. "*Neophyte Field Guide*," she read aloud. When she removed the book from the shelf, the remaining books collapsed like a set of dominoes. They fell perfectly into a set of steps. With a continuing thud, thud, the steps sank farther and farther into the floor, forming an underground passage. "Take the book, Robert. It contains valuable information. Whatever happens, do not lose it."

I turned from my fascination with the stairwell. Echoes rose to my ears from the books still clattering somewhere in the darkness below me. "Uh, yeah." I reached for the book.

"Now go. Follow the Stairway of Knowledge. You will learn much along the way. We have little time, no?"

Madame G. pointed to the steps.

"But, aren't you coming?" Though she repulsed me, Madame Gorgonzola was the closest thing I had to a friend here. Without her, who knew how long it would take me to get back home?

"No, young Robert. We all have our own duties. You may see me later. You will be in good hands. Make haste now." She shooed me toward the dark entrance.

I tentatively inched my way down a few of the steps. These books were about the size of my science textbook at school. I had always thought it was huge and heavy, but I'd never tried walking on it. I really had to tiptoe not to fall off the narrow stairway the books made.

"Farmhouse Cheddar makes many wounds better." A disembodied voice announced.

"What?" I turned back to see if Madame G. was giving last minute directions, but the entrance to the stairwell held only dust, swirling in a shaft of light from her office.

"Farmhouse Cheddar makes many wounds better." The words vibrated through the bottoms of my feet all the way into my brain. I looked down at the book. Carefully I picked up one foot and read the title words, *Cheese Monger*. I had to put my first foot down and pick up my other foot to get the rest of the title. *First Aid.* "*Cheese Monger First*

Aid?" I said aloud. What was a cheese monger? I'd have to ask someone next chance I got. I hoped I wouldn't need to give anybody first aid on this trip.

Farther in the deepening darkness of the passageway I heard, "Many monsters fear Muenster." My feet shook again while the words materialized inside my head. This time I stepped down a book to read the title under me, *Eradication of Monster Infestations*. First aid and monsters. This wasn't looking promising.

In a few more steps, I felt the familiar buzzing and heard, "Port Salut rids you of the hairy brute." Now I understood why Madame G. called this the "Stairway of Knowledge". Somehow, I needed this information. Monsters and hairy brutes did not sound good. Not good at all. How was I ever going to remember all this?

I started repeating the lines I had heard. "Farmhouse Cheddar makes many wounds better. Many monsters fear Muenster. Port Salut rids you of the hairy brute." I knew about Cheddar and Muenster, but what was "Port Salut"? Probably some weird cheese I had never heard of before. The book I stood on was entitled *Werewolves, Abominable Snowmen and other Hairy Beasts*. I was going to need all the help I could get. I repeated the lines of bad poetry as I continued my descent. They became easier to remember.

"The manticore flees at the smell of Limburger Cheese." Werewolves and monsters were scary enough. I had no idea about a manticore. I moved down a step and picked up the book that had buzzed me this time, *Monsters in Myth and Legend*. Hesitantly, I opened it. I skipped over many pages until I found the M's. On page 252, a grotesque creature stared at me. Its snarling human head held three rows of razor sharp teeth. The muscular lion body ended in a tail containing hundreds of sharp points. I read the description:

> *The manticore, an ancient creature, hails from Persia. Mentioned often by Greek and Roman authors, it has the ability to shoot poison darts from its tail. The manticore is swift and can leap tremendous distances. Its name means 'man-eater'. The manticore toys with its prey, asking riddles before devouring its prisoners whole.*

I definitely needed a good supply of Limburger. I replaced the book and looked ahead. The passage looked like it dead-ended in about five steps. I felt the familiar buzzing.

"The Drunken Goat of Spain brings you home again."
I imagined a goat stumbling down the road and laughed.
If I had to follow some crazy goat to get home, I would
do it. The book that provided this relevant information
was called *Cheese Transport: Improvements Through the
Centuries.*

At the last step, there was a small wooden door. I
pushed it lightly, and it swung open with a long, slow,
creak. I scanned the tiny dusty room filled with maps,
books, and shelf after shelf of cheeses, each carefully cata-
loged under its own dome. In the center of the room, an
empty dome sat on a pedestal. Blue light from somewhere
shone on the vacant space. I stood and stared at it. My
lungs inhaled the moldy basement smell. The damp air
made my skin feel cool and moist.

I heard a familiar voice, although I couldn't see anyone. "Welcome, Robert."

From the shadows, an old man materialized from thin
air, and I jumped and knocked my head on the beam of
the low ceiling. I rubbed the back of my head and stared
at him. He was the same man who had first defended me
in the lobby.

"I am Stefano Parmesan." He motioned to a chair
beside a small wooden table as he took the other chair.

"Quickly. Sit. Have you learned the secrets of the Syndicate?" He leaned forward and looked at me with interest.

"I think so," I said, hesitating.

"Recite them, please." He nodded toward me.

"Okay, I'll try." I counted out on my fingers as I listed them. "The Drunken Goat of Spain brings you home again. The manticore flees at the smell of Limburger cheese. Port Salut rids you of the hairy brute. Many monsters fear Muenster." I tapped my pinky against the table. I couldn't think of the first one. Something about Cheddar. I looked at Stefano. "I'm sorry. I can't remember any more." His disappointed look made me turn my eyes away and concentrate on the floor.

"Repeat after me," he said. "Farmhouse Cheddar makes many wounds better."

I did.

"We have no time for formal training. The secrets must suffice." He continued in a kind voice, "It is very important, Robert, for you to remember them. Let us practice."

I repeated the five "syndicate secrets" for what seemed like an hour.

"Stop." Stefano raised his hand. "I believe you shall not now forget them. Presently, you must attend to these maps." He unrolled two crumbling parchments and traced his bony finger through Europe to the Mediterranean Sea. I didn't know where he'd gotten them, but they looked like they were older than dirt. They had all sorts of writing on them that I didn't understand. Some of it didn't even look like letters, more like ancient symbols. "Eliki was a city in Greece many, many years ago," Stefano explained. "It fell into the sea during a great earthquake. Within the city was a huge statue of Poseidon."

"Poseidon?" I asked. I'd never heard of him.

"Yes, Poseidon, the Greek god of the sea. The Elikians worshipped him. You may know him by his Roman name, Neptune."

"Oh, yeah." I nodded as if I knew what he was talking about. Really, I wasn't too up on my mythology. I should have paid more attention during English class.

"We believe the lost cheese of Eliki was stored in the tip of Poseidon's trident. In legend, this cheese had great restorative powers. We are most anxious to find it. It may hold the key to a great many secrets."

"Is this the cheese that can fix up Janine?" I asked. I would've thought she'd need more than a bite of cheese to cure her ailments, but before today, I thought sisters couldn't shrink and cheese couldn't talk. What did I know?

"We believe it can, Robert." Stefano relaxed and smiled for the first time since I'd walked into the room.

I let out a deep sigh. "What do I have to do?"

"You must take these maps, find Eliki, get the cheese, and return here."

"Is that it?" I folded my arms and nodded my head. "No problem. No problem at all," I said with fake cheerfulness.

"Robert, reserve your wit for the quest. You shall need it." He frowned again at me and handed me a large hiking pack. "I have assembled a sack with everything you need. Consult your field manual when you are unsure about a course of action, and please, Robert, take notes as you go," he said, handing me a small notebook. "The Syndicate's researchers rely on our agents' field notes to develop new defenses against our enemies."

"You mean like homework?" I moaned. I couldn't get away from school, not even in this dank underground cave. Technically, I guess I was still in my room. In a cave, inside a bottle, in my bedroom. Yeah. This was weird.

"Robert, this is not an educational exercise. Your observations might make the difference between life and death for some future agent." Stefano's brows creased deeply as he bent his head toward me.

I thought about his words. "Accuracy is important?" I raised my eyebrows.

"Very important," he said, letting that smile creep back onto his somber face.

"Will there really be werewolves and stuff like that?" I looked at Stefano. I didn't want him to think I was a chicken, but on the other hand, I'd rather not meet any of those creatures I saw in the books on the stairwell.

"Just remember the secrets, and you will remain safe," he said, giving me a reassuring pat on the back.

"How am I supposed to get to Greece?" I asked while I stood up and stuffed the manual Madame Gorgonzola had given me, along with the notebook, into the fat, green backpack and strapped it on.

"Some cheeses have great powers, Robert," Stefano explained as he stood and replaced his chair. He walked along the rows of cheeses, waving his hand. "Assembled in this room you shall find every mystical cheese, save one."

"The mystic cheese of Eliki?" I guessed.

"Yes. It belongs under that central dome." Stefano nodded toward the pedestal in the center of the room.

I remembered that I needed to find out about cheese mongers, in case one of them needed first aid. "Stefano, what's a cheese monger?" I asked.

"Come now, Robert." He smiled through his cracked face. "Do you not know what a cheese monger is?"

"Sorry, I really don't." I shook my head.

"You are a cheese monger, Robert. As is your father," he replied. "Everyone in the syndicate is a cheese monger."

"I am?" I shook my head. That explanation didn't help me much but it didn't seem like Stefano was going to elaborate. He turned away and walked along the row of cheeses. "From this portal, the cheeses present can take you anywhere in the world, if you eat the proper one." His eyes continued to scan the shelves as he tapped his finger on his chin. "Hmm, for Greece, I think you need Greek Kasseri." He rummaged along the shelves in a far corner and found the appropriate dome. After removing the glass, he sliced a small piece. "Here, eat this and you shall be on your way."

I brought the cheese to my mouth.

"Wait!" Stefano commanded in such a sharp tone that I dropped the cheese. I thought I'd done something wrong. "I almost forgot." He brought his hand up to his chest. "You must take Janine."

"Janine?" I moaned as I picked up the piece of Kasseri. "She's here?" I spun around looking for her.

Stefano nodded. He removed a miniature dollhouse

from his shirt pocket and handed it to me. I put it up to my eye and squinted. I could barely make her out waving to me from the window.

"Hey, Robert!" Her squeaky voice was still incredibly irritating. "Isn't this cool? I've shrunk. I've got my own house and everything. It's got a computer, TV, and my own MP3 player. I don't need to borrow yours anymore. Mr. Stefano told me they built this whole thing just for me. It's practically indestructible. I'm snug as a bug. Don't worry about me."

I smiled in spite of my irritation with her. She continued yapping, and I tucked her safely into my pocket.

"We've given Janine a temporary antidote and she will not shrink much more for the next twenty-four hours," Stefano explained. "If, however, you do not retrieve the cheese before that time, the process will continue until she is a mere atom."

I had only twenty-four hours. Piece of cake. "Why can't you just give her the antidote again?" I asked.

"If only there were time to explain," Stefano said with a grimace. "Come, Robert. You must make haste." Stefano shook my hand and took a step back. "Good luck. The Syndicate is counting on you."

There's nothing like the weight of grown-up expectations

to add a little pressure. I gulped down the cheese, expecting another swirling experience like my trip into the bottle, but everything just went black.

Chapter 5

Somewhere in the Darkness

I floated, sailed, or sped—it's hard to say which—through a dark void. I saw nothing. When I screamed, my ears heard nothing. I didn't smell or touch anything. I might have slept, but it's hard to say. If I were a scientist, I might have said I was in a black hole, but instead, I thought I was dead.

Time passed. It could have been hours or days. Then, suddenly the black hole spit me out. *Thump!*

"Ow!" Surprised at my own voice, I stood up and rubbed my backside. Stuff fell out of my backpack all over the ground. "Oh, great!" I said to no one in particular.

I'd forgotten to zip it, and it must have twisted upside down during my zero gravity space ride. I felt around on the ground for things and started to shove them back into the pack. I hoped I got it all because I still couldn't see a thing. Stefano hadn't even bothered to pack a flashlight. Maybe he thought I had cat eyes and could see in the dark.

Even though it was pitch black, the solid ground beneath my feet reassured me. I gazed up into a starry sky. I was in a small clearing, surrounded by the shadows of dense trees. At least I was back on earth somewhere, hopefully Greece.

I walked forward a few steps, tripped over a rock, fell back down, and hit my lip on an exposed root. I spit out dirt, grass, and a little salty blood. So far, this was some kind of quest. After I rolled over, I decided to wait until morning to move. Otherwise, I might kill myself without even meeting a monster.

"Man, it's dark out here." Janine's tiny voice reached my ears.

"What are you doing? You're going to get lost in the dark." I couldn't see her, but I felt her climbing out of my pocket. It tickled when she walked across my chest.

"I'm hungry," Janine complained. She was always hungry.

"Don't you have any food in your house?"

"I did, but I ate it. We were on the "Lost in Space" channel for a really long time." Janine thinks anything longer than ten minutes is a long time.

I reached into my pocket and pulled out a stick of gum. "Here. It's all I have for now. It's too dark to see anything in my backpack, and I'm not letting you eat any of that Syndicate stuff 'til I get a good look at it."

"Robert, this gum is as big as me!" she squeaked.

"Oh, sorry. I guess you are pretty small." I broke off a tiny piece. "Take this." I put my finger somewhere close to my pocket.

"Thanks." I felt her take the gum. Despite her tiny size, I could still hear her smacking. Janine chews gum like a cow.

"Now, go back inside," I ordered.

"You're not the boss of me, Robert Montasio. I think I'll sit out here with you for a while."

"Whatever," I moaned. "But I'm just going to hang out until morning. Then I'll be able to see where I'm going." Using my pack as a pillow, I stretched out on the ground. I felt Janine strumming her fingers against my chest. She'd be a good drummer if she tried. It was irritating, like a tiny gnat crawling around on my skin, but I kept quiet.

"This is exciting," Janine announced after about thirty seconds. "I'm going back to watch TV."

"See you later, sis." I knew she wouldn't stay out with me too long if I didn't do anything. Janine never could sit still. Janine never sits at all. She dances. She jumps. She skips. She's like that bunny on TV with the batteries that never wear out. She never shuts up, either. I called her "Motor Mouth" when we were little.

On long car trips, Mom and Dad always resorted to bribery for a little peace and quiet. It didn't matter what they promised her. Money. Candy. New clothes. Once, they promised her a new pony, a real live one, complete with the pink and purple saddle and beads for its mane. She didn't get it. She never, ever, got the reward because she couldn't last more than five minutes without opening her mouth and telling us her latest, exciting discovery.

The stars were shinier here than at home. Less light pollution, I guessed. Of course, it was difficult to say where "here" was. I was in the middle of nowhere and lost in the Greek countryside. Technically, I might still be inside the Effervescent Elixir bottle. If that was true, Janine wasn't the only one who'd shrunk. I gave up trying to figure it out and looked back up at the stars.

They twinkled so brightly in the black sky above me that I felt as though I could touch them. Involuntarily my arm moved upward. The stars danced around my fingers. It made me dizzy, like on a roller coaster. They moved closer to me. I bolted upright. These were not stars. They were some kind of insect, like fireflies. What if they stung? Oh, I so hated bugs. Every muscle in my body tensed up while they spun around my head, faster and faster. I froze.

"Stop!" I finally yelled because I couldn't take it any-more. To my surprise, they listened and hovered about two feet above my eyes. I could see now that they weren't bugs. They were tiny people, like pixies or fairies, with lu-minescent wings. They stared expectantly at me.

"Who are you?" I whispered, still afraid to move.

They erupted into high-pitched laughter. I didn't see what was so funny.

"Who are you?" I asked again.

"Friend or foe? Friend or foe? He does not know. He does not know. If he must ask, he may not pass." They chanted in squeaky voices, slowly circling my head.

"I'm a friend," I started to say. I tried to duck my head out of their circle, but they moved in unison with me. They weren't going to let me out of their ring.

"How rude, how rude. Oh what a shame. He doesn't first give us his name." They interrupted me, continuing their song as they chased each other around my head. The night got noticeably brighter as more of them joined the swarm.

I felt my heart thudding as they darted faster and closer to my face with each pass. They pointed their fin-gers and shouted about my name. I didn't know what to do. Stefano never mentioned anything like this. I decided to take a chance.

"I am Robert Montasio," I blurted out.

"Oooh!" They fell silent and drew back slightly. Impressed by their reaction, I continued. "I'm searching for the lost city of Eliki," I said in a louder voice.

"Ahh!" They retreated another wingspan.

"Can you help me?" My pulse started to come back down to normal. It looked like they weren't going to hurt me after all.

"We know your name." One of the bigger fairies flew forward. He was about the size of a wasp. "We are the Anerada. We will help you. I am Teeree, special liaison to all Syndicate agents."

"How'd you know I'm part of the Syndicate?" I asked, completely dumbfounded.

"Montasio is a name of great power and renown among the Anerada," he explained.

"Cool." I felt a smile spread across my face in the dark. I had no idea my family was so famous. To me, we were just us, the Montasios from New Jersey. I wished Dad had told us something about our history.

"It is good you finally gave your name to my people. We were prepared to perform the light spin, which would have left you helpless, maybe even dead." I couldn't tell if he was joking. Probably not.

"Oh." My smile quickly vanished. I couldn't think of anything else to say. Apparently, there was a great deal Stefano left out of my training. "Can you help me find Eliki?" I asked. The Anerada slowly dispersed while we talked, leaving us again in darkness.

"Yes," Teeree said. "Let us be on our way. I must dim myself so we do not attract any unwanted attention." With that, his light faded until he seemed like the glowing embers of a dying campfire. After my eyes adjusted, I followed him. He flitted deftly between the trees, finding the surest path. I trotted to keep up. My feet stirred up a foggy mist every time one of my sneakers hit the ground.

We traveled wordlessly for about an hour, until the trees began to thin. I noticed the land rising as we neared the edge of the forest. Teeree stopped short at the crest of a hilltop and pointed into the darkness. "Beyond this rise, the land falls down to the sea. We are near the edge of the Forest of Darkness."

"Forest of Darkness?" I asked.

"Yes. Cheese travelers always arrive in a Dark Forest. We guide them out. Are you sure you are a Montasio?" I heard the skepticism in his voice, but I couldn't see his face.

"Yeah. Let's just say I haven't had the full training course. Do you have any other advice for me?" I figured anything he could help me with would cut down on my learning curve.

"Yes." He started to tell me something, and then he stopped, holding a barely perceptible finger up to his lips. "Wait. Listen." Whatever he was listening to, I couldn't hear.

"Run, Robert. As fast as you can. A great danger approaches. You will be safe when you reach the light. I will deal with this beast."

"Wait!" I cried. "What is it? Will I see you again?" Everything was going so well a second ago. Then, BAM! I was going to be on my own against whatever it was coming through the woods. It wasn't fair.

"Robert, you must listen. This beast is a chimera, and it is very dangerous. It searches for you. Now go." Teeree spun and flew quickly back up the path. In a moment, I lost sight of him.

A great crashing sound reached my ears. The thing behind us was big. From the trees in the distance, wailing screams rose into the night, and I forced myself to turn and look. A huge beast, about twice as big as me, roared and snapped at a little dot of light. That must have been

Teeree. I saw the beast's outline as fire shot, like daggers, from its mouth. Teeree blazed brighter as he spun to avoid the flames. Go, Teeree!

Each time it tried to roast Teeree, I got another glimpse. It had a shaggy lion head and some kind of animal body. There was another head coming out of the middle of the body, but I couldn't tell what kind of animal it was. It whipped a dragon tail back and forth, trying to knock Teeree from the sky.

The chimera lifted its lion head and spotted me. I willed my feet to move but they remained frozen to the ground. A column of fire climbed into the sky, and I saw the middle head turn towards me. It had some horns— maybe it was a goat. The tail looked at me too. Ugh! The tail had its own head. It was the head of a snake, with huge fangs. The whole thing was hideous.

"Montasio!" All three heads screamed into the night. "You will fail! We will see to that!" Teeree got in a flash of something that must have made it very angry, because the chimera turned from me and swatted Teeree with his huge snakehead tail. I saw Teeree's speck of light sail off as though he'd been hit with a baseball bat. My stomach tied itself into a knot. What had happened to Teeree? I wanted to run after him, but my legs had turned to gelatin.

The chimera turned its heads again toward me. "You are mine now!" Its three pairs of eyes locked onto mine and I understood, for the very first time, the danger I was in.

"Robert!" Janine pounded on my chest. "We've got to go!"

"What?" I managed to look away for a minute.

"Now, Robert!" she screamed at me. "We've got to go NOW!"

She was right. I had stayed too long. Stupid. Stupid. Wrenching myself away, I pumped my legs faster and faster. Vines and brush scratched me as I rushed by. I didn't look back again, but I heard the chimera's growling as he chased me. The ground pounded beneath my feet, matching the pounding in my brain. Soon, multicolored bits of light brightened the darkness. They flew past me with amazing speed. The other Anerada were flying in to help!

I hoped they were strong enough to hold off that chimera until I got out of the woods. Maybe they would do their light spin. It would serve him right. I never did anything to him. I'd never even met him before. Why did he hate me so much? My head swam with questions. I prayed Teeree was all right. I knew there was nothing I could do to help him.

I slowed for just a moment to sneak one peek back. A wall of rainbow stripes spun like a cyclone about fifty yards behind me. I doubted anything could get beyond that column of light. All right, Anerada! They'd show that chimera a thing or two.

"Robert!" Janine yelled again. "Come on! We aren't out of the woods yet."

She was right again, but I didn't have enough breath to tell her that. I turned again and continued running. Soon I passed the edge of the hill and started toward the seashore. The trees and vines gave way to waist-high bushes and grasses. The dim, grey light appeared to be the dawning of the day.

When I reached the seashore, I collapsed on the beach. Neither man nor beast was in sight. Sweat poured from my arms and legs, making sand stick all over me. My mouth felt like a shriveled prune. I could hear my heart thumping. I didn't know where I was going, and my guide was somewhere behind me, probably dead. This secret agent stuff wasn't nearly as much fun as it seemed in the movies.

Chapter 6

On the Beach

I must have fallen asleep on the sand because I dreamt Janine called me. I could hear her obnoxious voice, something about washing up. A buzzing sound in my ear woke me. I shook my head violently, thinking a bee was about to sting. The bee sailed out of my ear, landing softly in the sand.

"Ewww! Gross!" Janine's voice made me open my eyes. Too bad this entire day wasn't just a bad dream. Janine wrinkled her nose and threw up her hands. "Robert, when's the last time you cleaned out your ears? How can you hear anything with all that wax in there?" She pulled her tiny self up from the sand and dusted off her jeans.

I squinted at her with a frown on my face. "Janine, why aren't you in your house?" I turned over and brought my head close to her, propping it up on my elbow. She seemed smaller than ever.

"I got bored. I kept trying to wake you up, but you sleep like a rock. So I climbed up to your ear and yelled.

That got your attention." She gave me a smug grin, climbed nimbly onto my arm, and plopped down onto her back. Her squeaky little voice, unfortunately, did not decrease in volume. Its higher pitch, however, irritated me more than I'd thought possible.

"I thought you were a bee," I explained.

"Well, I'm still bored. What do you think happened to Teeree? He was so cute. When you two started running I felt like I was on a trampoline inside your pocket. So he should have been back by now, don't you think?" Janine finally stopped to breathe. Before I could open my mouth, she started up again. "And what was that nasty thing yelling at you? He looked like something straight out of those old scary movies. If I hadn't gotten you going, he'd have flame-broiled us for sure."

I stared at her, incredulous. Nothing about last night fazed her at all. "Janine, I don't know what happened to Teeree. I was running to get away from that thing. It was a chimera. Teeree held it back so I could escape."

"Well, you should have left a little sooner, don't you think?" Janine scolded me, oblivious to our predicament.

"Janine!" I screamed at her. "We're lost on a beach. I don't even know what day it is. Mom's probably at home by now freaking out. Soon, you'll be shrinking again by the minute. We have to find Eliki. We have to find Dad. Nobody's here to help us, and I don't know what to do!" I glared at her. She glared back at me. "This is all your fault, you know." I folded my arms and tried to stare her down.

"No way," she shook her head, "I heard the cheese guys in Madame Gorgonzola's office. Bet you didn't know I was there, huh? You're in charge, so everything is your fault. If you're going to be mean, I'm going back to my house." With hands on her hips, she huffed up my arm and climbed toward my pocket.

"And another thing," she shouted before disappearing into the pocket, "don't you have some sort of instruction book? Why don't you read it? Duh!" I heard her tiny front door slam.

The manual. Why hadn't I thought of it? I forgot how aggravated I was and dug through the backpack.

I found an apple. My stomach grumbled, reminding me that I was starving, so I ate it. Finding some cheese, I started in on that. It was pretty good. I turned over the cheese and looked at the label. Farmhouse Cheddar. I stopped chewing. This was one of the five secret cheeses. I might need it later. I carefully wrapped the remainder and put it away. Hopefully, I hadn't eaten too much of it.

"I better recite the secrets," I said aloud. No one

answered, so I started.

"Farmhouse Cheddar makes many wounds better. Many monsters fear Muenster. The manticore flees at the smell of Limburger cheese. Port Salut rids you of the hairy brute. The Drunken Goat of Spain brings you home again." I smiled to myself, knowing I still had command of the Syndicate's secrets.

I reached into the pack again and pulled out the rest of the junk. I didn't know what any of it did. To my horror, I realized that the manual wasn't there. What had happened to it? Madame Gorgonzola had said to make sure I didn't lose it. I'd screwed up again. I threw myself down on the sand next to a big boulder. Now I had no idea what to do. Janine wasn't talking to me, and I was stuck here. I didn't even know where "here" was. Could things get any worse? Probably, but I didn't see how.

The sun rose higher in the sky as I leaned against the rock and stared out at the waves. My empty brain gave me no help. I sat in silence.

Moments later, I jumped as a big, black, wet nose sniffed my ear. Every muscle in my body tensed as it sniffed my hair on the back of my head. It moved around to sniff my face, and I saw that it was a huge, white dog. It kept sniffing my shirt and my pants. I was afraid to move because it didn't look very friendly. It must have been some sort of working dog because it had a set of saddlebags across its back.

After an eternity of sniffing every part of me, it sat back and stared at me with dark, disapproving eyes. I got the feeling it didn't really like me. The dog must have had an owner somewhere. Without moving my head, I tried to scan the beach and edge of the forest, looking for someone to call it off. I didn't want to add a dog bite to my list of problems for today.

"Who are you looking for?" it growled at me.

A talking dog. This shouldn't have surprised me, based on everything else that had happened recently, but it did. I stared at it, not knowing what to say.

"Are you mute, boy?" it growled again. "Speak up."

"No. I, I just didn't expect you to talk. I've never met a dog who could speak."

"There is so little you know, boy. I am Skylos, protector of this territory. My time has been wasted this morning, searching for you. Answer my question now. Are you Robert Montasio?"

"Yes, I am," I said, amazed again that so many creatures seemed to know me. "Why are you looking for me?" My muscles relaxed a little, and I let my legs slide down.

"Reach into my pouch. I have something I think you need." Skylos stood up so I could get what he had for me. I didn't move. "Come on, boy. Are you dimwitted?" he growled. "I have other things to do this day."

I reached over his head, slowly, past his sharp, gleaming teeth and stuck my hand into the pocket of his bag. I pulled out a book. "My *Field Guide*!" I shouted. "Where'd you find it?"

"I did not find it," Skylos said with a sniff. "I am simply delivering it for you. You must be more careful with your things. Next time you lose it, you might not be so lucky. It could have fallen into the wrong hands." Skylos sounded like my mother lecturing me about picking up my dirty socks.

"But who?" I started to ask.

"I have no time for explanations," Skylos growled again. "I must continue my patrol." With that, he turned and trotted down the beach.

"Thank you, Skylos," I called after him. He flicked his tail at me. I guessed that was a wave goodbye. My *Neophyte Field Guide*. I wondered if the Anerada had found it. I'd probably never know. The thought of that ugly chimera getting a hold of it made me shudder. Now wasn't the time to think about that. The important thing was that I had it back. I opened the field manual and turned to the table of contents.

Traveling Through the Void . . . . . . *p. 4*
Negotiating the Dark Forests. . . . . . *p. 7*
Passage through Neptune's Realm . . . *p. 9*

I didn't bother to look at the rest. Neptune was the same as the Poseidon fellow Stefano had mentioned. I was at the sea. I didn't have a boat, and I needed to get across. I turned to page nine, ready to get on with the rest of the quest.

After a few minutes of reading, I figured out that I had to find a conch shell, blow it three times while facing east, ask for the help of Triton's legions, and wait to see what showed up. That didn't seem too hard. Triton, it turned out, was the son of Poseidon, or Neptune, depending on if you were doing the Greek or Roman mythology thing. Maybe he was like a prince of the sea or something. This book was quite the mythology lesson. It even had a nice picture of a conch shell to help me out. That was good, because I had no idea what a conch looked like.

I walked down the beach, spotting bits of flotsam along the way. There were whole and broken sand dollars, cool butterfly shells in pink, yellow, and purple, gnarled driftwood pieces, and assorted other bits of refuse that had floated in with the tide. Finally, I spotted a conch shell. It was kind of small, but I figured it would do.

I grabbed it by the spikes that radiated from the top of its spiral and turned it over in my hand. How did you blow a conch shell? Was it supposed to whistle? I didn't really know, so I faced east, put the tip to my lips and blew. It didn't make any noise. I looked out into the sea. Nothing happened so I blew again. Still I didn't see any of Triton's legions. I blew it once more. Nothing. What was wrong? Then I remembered. I'd forgotten to ask for help.

I faced the sea and called out, "Mighty Triton, I need your aid." Before I had time to feel foolish, the foam of the gently breaking waves rose up into what looked like, for lack of a better word, a merman. He had wildly curling hair and a long beard made from the bubbling surf. His body was a translucent green, with eyes that reflected the light like crystals.

"Who disturbs Triton's rest?" the watery merman boomed out in a rich voice.

Having learned a thing or two from the Anerada, I boldly stepped forward. While trying to deepen my own voice, I said, "It is I, Robert Montasio, Agent of the Secret

Cheese Syndicate." Too bad, my voice cracked at the end, and I croaked out the word "Syndicate" like a sick frog. Triton looked at me and laughed, spraying me with surf. This was not going as I planned. The Anerada had been so impressed when I mentioned my name. I didn't know what else to do.

"I am Robert Montasio." I stepped closer to the water, hoping he would take me seriously this time.

"You are a Montasio. That much I see. You are but a boy. Go home." His body began receding into the surf.

"Wait!" I shouted, reaching out to him. "Madame Gorgonzola sent me on this quest. Please help me!" I pleaded with him. He turned to gaze at me. It was so strange because only his head was still above the water. He reminded me of those disembodied ghost heads, floating around in the air. My fingers tingled when he talked. My hair stood on end. Just one more creepy, weird, strange encounter to add to today's list.

"Why would Madame Gorgonzola send one so young to my shores?"

"I need to find the lost cheese of Eliki," I said hopefully.

"But why?" Triton's body rose again from the surf. Fully formed, he crossed his translucent arms.

Involuntarily, my foot dug into the wet sand while I

thought about what to say. Water continually flowed back into the depression, undoing my work. I could dig like this forever and never get anywhere. Finally, I made a decision and looked up at Triton. I went with the truth.

"Because I let my sister drink a bottle of Madame G.'s elixir, and now she's shrinking, and I want to find my father," I said. I stood up straight, waiting to hear him complain about my irresponsibility and lack of experience.

Instead, Triton rubbed his foamy beard and stared straight through me. "You wish to right your wrong?" His words came out slowly. I felt like he was considering my worthiness.

"Yes," I nodded, "and find my father," I added, my heart racing.

"Madame Gorgonzola thinks you can do this?"

"She said I was her last hope." I was glad she'd said that. I don't think Triton would have believed me if I tried to lie to him about anything dealing with the Syndicate.

"Very well, my soldiers will bear you," he said.

"Thanks," I said, relaxing my shoulders a little.

The merman nodded and turned toward the sea. He whistled a high-pitched vibration, which spread across the water, creating a small ripple wave before it. Almost instantly, his "soldiers" showed up, clicking and chattering.

"Cool, dolphins!" Janine climbed up on my shoulder.

"How long have you been listening?" I had to look down my nose to see her.

"Since forever. I hear everything from inside your pocket."

"Oh." I wanted to apologize for yelling at her earlier, but I didn't.

"What are you waiting for?" She pointed toward the dolphins. "Let's go for a ride."

For once, I liked one of Janine's ideas.

Chapter 7

Into Neptune's Realm

I turned back to thank Triton, but saw only his hair disappearing into the surf. He sure didn't like to hang around long. I waded into the water. The biggest dolphin nodded his head, beckoning me. I took that as a good sign and walked toward him.

"He's beautiful," Janine gushed.

Around seven feet long, his shiny grey skin glistened with ocean wetness. I felt the gaze of his piercing black eyes. He was magnificent. He extended a flipper. I eagerly reached out to touch it. It was silky smooth, yet very firm at the same time. I could not let go.

"Welcome to Neptune's Realm, Robert." A nasal voice from nowhere permeated my brain. I looked around. There was no one there. I looked at the dolphin. He nodded again, knowingly.

"I am Delfini, captain of Triton's command."

"How'd you do that?" I understood Delfini was talking, but I didn't know how.

"Do what?" he said.

"Talk without making a sound."

"Humans!" Delfini made a series of clicks. I think he was laughing. "My race can communicate simply by touch."

"You're telepathic?"

"Not exactly. We must be in physical contact, but telepathy is the best way for you to understand it."

"Robert, are you talking to that dolphin? I can't hear him," Janine whined, interrupting. "I want to talk to the dolphin."

"Janine, go back into the house. You're going to fall into the water." I didn't want her interfering with my conversation.

"No!"

"Janine!"

"Perhaps you should let her speak with me for a moment," Delfini suggested.

"All right." I reluctantly dropped his flipper and held out my palm for Janine. "Hop up here, I'll put you where you can touch Delfini and talk to him."

Janine reached out to touch the dolphin, balancing herself by grabbing onto my thumb.

"Thanks Delfini," she said. She nodded her head

several times and smiled. A moment later she said, "I'll try." I couldn't hear anything Delfini said since I wasn't touching him.

Janine turned to me. "I'm ready to go back into your pocket now, Robert."

"What'd he say to you?"

"None of your business." She made the "loser" L on her forehead with her thumb and index finger. "Let's get cracking. We've got a far way to go."

Janine still had her standard level of nastiness for me, but whatever Delfini said had worked wonders for her cooperation level. I brought my hand back to my pocket and Janine jumped off, disappearing into its folds without putting up a bit of a fight. I turned back to Delfini and grabbed his flipper again.

"Climb onto my back. We must make haste."

Riding on the dolphin was almost indescribable. He moved so fast and yet, the ride was so smooth. No bumps. No jolts. He slid through the water, just beneath the surface, and I felt like I was gliding on ice. His powerful muscles rippled under me. I remembered thinking we were cloud jumping every time he sailed through the air.

Delfini spoke very little to me, except to describe the occasional sea creature we passed, but he chattered constantly to the dolphin cohort. I had no idea what they said, but it didn't seem important. Their conversation was happy. I was happy. Last night seemed like a bad dream.

"Robert," Delfini's vibrating voice roused me from my thoughts.

"Yes."

"Look to the far shore. Do you see the mountain rising in the distance?"

I strained my eyes. "Just barely. You must have great eyesight."

"Not really. But I know where I am, and I can sense the mountain's base under the sea floor. That is the Mountain of Eliki."

"Really?" I asked, surprised.

"Yes. The lost city is buried beneath it."

"Beneath it? How am I supposed to get to it?" I felt a little tingle of fear shoot through me at the idea of going underground. I'm kind of claustrophobic.

"The mountain is a long dead volcano. You will need to descend into the crater and seek out a passage leading downward."

"Can't you come with me?" I hoped Delfini would bring me straight to the city through some underwater cave. I felt safe with him.

"Do not be afraid, Robert. You have done well to come this far," Delfini reassured me.

"You think so?" I said, glad that somebody finally found something other than criticism for me.

"Yes. There is help inside the mountain."

"Help?" I questioned.

"Look for the mountain gnome. He will guide you truly, but not willingly."

"What do you mean, not willingly?"

"You must first offer a gift," Delfini instructed.

"What kind of gift?"

"The gnome men are greedy little beasts. Human food is a delicacy for them, as they ordinarily eat rock and dirt."

"I've got lots of cheese," I said.

"That will do, but do not let them trick you out of your entire supply," he cautioned me.

Without warning, a host of dolphin chatterings interrupted our conversation. Delfini began zigzagging through the water, moving faster than I thought possible.

"Delfini, what's wrong?" My heartbeat quickened with his movements.

"Robert, an ozaena has picked up our scent. We must evade him at all costs. Hold tightly now. I may dive, but will not stay under the water very long. How long can you hold your breath?"

"I'm good for about a minute, but what about Janine?"

"She will be safe. Her house is both water and fire-proof."

That was good information to know. "Is an ozaena a monster?"

"Yes. It's a filthy creature, a leviathan that lives on the ocean bottom, in the dark places," Delfini said. I could feel the disgust in his voice.

"Stefano gave me some Muenster cheese. Will that help?" I asked.

"Perhaps. Get it quickly. You may need it if I can't shake the beast. I shall slow down for a second." I hugged Delfini tightly with my legs while I dug through my pack and found the Muenster. It came attached to a string loop, which I placed on my wrist.

"Got it!" I yelled. No sooner had I done this than Delfini sped off again. I grabbed his dorsal fin just in time.

I heard a loud bellowing behind us. As I turned to look, a huge creature broke the ocean surface. It looked more like a plant than an animal. Its body was long and cylindrical. Covered in green trailing slime, it reminded me of a cucumber that had been in the back of the fridge for too long. It had a gaping hole on one end. I supposed that was its mouth.

Delfini dove. I closed my eyes to keep out the salt water. It felt like we were somersaulting under the waves. I was almost out of breath, but I could do nothing but hang on. Finally, Delfini surfaced again, and I gasped in fresh air. I looked back.

The ozaena had gained on us. Its gigantic mouth wildly waved sucker-like tentacles toward us. That mouth could have easily swallowed us whole. Its bad breath made me nauseous. I grabbed tighter to Delfini's dorsal fin so I wouldn't fall off.

"The cheese, Robert." I heard Delfini's voice inside my head. "Get ready. I don't think I can swim faster than him."

I took the Muenster off my wrist, removing its wrappings. Whoa. It smelled as bad as the ozaena. "Delfini, can you spin around and head toward it? Then I'll throw the cheese into its mouth."

"I can do that, but be certain not to miss." I heard a tinge of doubt in his reply. Delfini circled wide right and came around one hundred and eighty degrees. As we sped closer to the mouth, I hoped all my free throw shooting would pay off. I lobbed the cheese in from about twenty feet away. A perfect shot.

The effect was spectacular. The ozaena shrieked and groaned the instant the Muenster hit. It crashed from side to side across the ocean surface, like a fish flopping on the floor. I guess it was trying to get rid of the cheese. Finally, it vomited out its guts and lay still. I think I just had my first monster kill. An oil slick of green and yellow mucous covered the ocean surface around the ozaena's body.

Soon sea snakes broke the greasy water surface. There must have be thousands of them. They gave me the creeps.

"Delfini, what are those things?" I asked. I really wanted to go, but I didn't want to seem like a coward.

"Those are the eels of the deep," Delfini explained. "They may look ferocious, but they will not harm you."

"What are they doing?" I let out a deep breath as I watched them churn and boil through the innards of the dead ozaena.

"They are ridding the ocean of the ozaena's venom. All creatures of the deep despise the ozaena. Its poison, if left unchecked, would spread throughout the seas and contaminate everything it touched."

"Cool. Like a big hazardous waste cleanup crew." I nodded my head.

"We must go now, Robert." Delfini quickly took me to the shore. I didn't want our journey to end, but I had to find the missing cheese. After I dismounted, I stood looking at him.

"Thank you, sir," I said shyly. Delfini and the other dolphins laughed in their familiar clicking way again. He put out his flipper once more.

"Robert, I am not a sir. I am a 'her'."

I laughed at my mistake.

"You must go now, Robert. Do not be sad at our parting. We may meet again another day."

"I hope so," I said, releasing her flipper. As I turned to go, the entire cohort rose out of the water, dancing backward on their tails. They sank into the deep, leaving the unbroken ocean to sparkle silver in the afternoon sunlight.

"Well, I guess that was another adventure I missed," Janine squeaked from my pocket.

"Yeah, it really was." I turned toward the mountain to begin the next part of the trip.

Chapter 8

Journey to the Crater

The ground rose steadily from the beach. The sandy shore disappeared behind us as we made our way up the only visible path. I stopped about a hundred yards in. I wanted to consult my *Neophyte Field Guide* before heading up the mountain. My soggy backpack dripped on my feet as I opened it. Everything inside was damp but looked okay. I rummaged through all the cheeses and other stuff, looking for the book.

"Oh, no!"

"What is it?" Janine asked.

"Some of my cheeses are gone," I wailed.

"Which ones? Maybe you don't need them anyway."

"I don't know." I dumped everything out on the ground. "We'd better take inventory." I piled up the cheeses in their categories. "Cheddar. Five wheels. That's good," I said. "Muenster, plenty of that." I tossed six hunks into another heap. "Port Salut, only two of those." I tossed around several wheels of cheese whose names I didn't recognize. "Great. Just great." I picked up the last wheel and threw it on the pile.

"What's missing?" Janine looked over the stacks of cheeses.

"I don't have any Limburger."

"What was that rhyme about Limburger?" she asked.

"The manticore flees at the smell of Limburger cheese," I moaned.

"Aww." Janine gloated. "We can outsmart a manticore any old day."

"Janine, you didn't see the picture of that manticore in the book. If we run into one of those guys, we'll be dog food."

"Well, maybe we won't meet any manticores," Janine said brightly. "How'd you lose it anyway?"

"Janine, I don't know." I threw up my hands. "It was kind of a hairy ride getting away from that ozaena. Maybe it fell out when I opened the pack to get the Muenster."

"We better go back to the beach, then. Maybe Delfini or one of the dolphins found it."

"Good idea, Janine." I was glad we weren't fighting anymore.

I turned around to retrace my steps. About halfway down the path toward the beach, I saw something coming up toward us. It was Skylos. He didn't look happy. As he got closer, I realized he was all wet. Not only that, but green slime covered his beautiful white fur.

"Uh oh," Janine said.

"Uh oh is right," I told her. "I wonder what he wants."

"Who do you think he is anyway?" Janine whispered.

"I don't know, but I don't think he likes us," I replied. "Maybe he found the cheese?"

Skylos had reached us now. Wow. I covered my nose. Those ozaena guts stunk.

"Robert Montasio," he growled and looked down his nose at me. I wanted to curl up in a ball. "Please retrieve your items from my pouch."

"Skylos, I'm sorry you had to get all . . ." I stopped. He smelled worse than a sewer. "Thanks for getting my stuff back," I said and reached into his pouch. Cold, green gook slimed me as I took the cheeses out. I tried to hold them as far away from me as I could.

He sniffed the air and turned around, his head and tail held high. "Robert Montasio," he growled over his shoulder as he trotted back down the path. "Do not lose anything else. I mean it."

"You know," Janine said. "He is so different from Bella. I wouldn't mind having a dog like him."

75

I laughed. "Janine, I don't think a dog like him wants an owner. Do you?"

"No, probably not. Hey, you've got to do something about that cheese. It's gross."

"I know. I think I've got a rag somewhere in here," I said and looked through my stuff again. "Here it is." I pulled out a piece of cheesecloth. It figured. What other kind of rag would Stefano use?

After I wiped the slime off the cheese, it didn't smell as bad. I counted it up, seven hunks of Limburger.

I didn't know what to do with the stinky cloth, so I hid it under some bushes. I didn't like littering, but there was no way it was coming with us. Besides, I figured that covered with all those Ozeana entrails, it would decompose into fertilizer in no time at all.

I stuffed the Limburger, and everything else, back into my pack. Last was my guide. I opened it up, and the pages weren't even wet.

"Janine, how cool is that? It's dry."

"Way cool," she said.

I walked up the path to the foot of the mountain. Here I stopped and consulted the guide. I turned to page eleven and found a chapter about mountain gnomes. It said:

*These tricksters exist in most of the an-
cient peaks. They honor their alliance of old
to our Syndicate, but they are not especially
friendly. Be careful not to offend them in
any way. They are very vain, and it is best
not to mention anything about their appearance, as this will cost you in the end. Pass
through their outlands quickly and with as
little disturbance as possible. If you do, their
sentries will not hinder you. You will begin
to notice these sentries hidden along your
path as you ascend the mountain. When you
reach the summit and need a guide into a
cave, call upon the name of Gob, the King
of the People of the Mountain. This should
produce a captain who will assist you, for a
price. Once you have driven a bargain you
can trust the gnome with your life, until he
has fulfilled his pledge.*

I closed the book and scanned the mountain ahead
of me. Somewhere up there was my next guide, but I
could see no sign of him. The rocky outcroppings showed
the layers of millions of years. Rosy and creamy stripes

in the boulders reminded me of the Neapolitans at Dad's restaurant.

Dad. I wondered where he was. Would I ever find him? Not if I didn't get started. I put the book into my pack and made sure to buckle it before I started walking again.

Janine dangled her arms over the edge of my pocket, looking at the scenery.

"Hey, Janine," I said, "do you remember how Francesca used to bake all those cool desserts at the restaurant?"

"Yeah," she sighed. "When Dad let me go in on Saturday mornings, she'd always have a special one hidden for me."

"Hey, me too! But she had to hide them from Bernhardt. She always made me eat mine in the big pantry so he didn't find out that she'd given me one."

"Bernie never liked you." She laughed. "But he always pulled mints from behind my ear before I left. He was a great magician."

"Are you kidding?" I couldn't believe Dad's maitre d' would give away anything, or waste time with magic tricks on little kids. He always shooed me out of everywhere at the restaurant, and he watched me like a hawk to make sure I didn't snitch food.

"I miss going to Dad's restaurant," Janine said, staring at the ground as she bounced in my pocket.

"Yeah. I miss Dad, too." I walked on in silence for a while, thinking about Dad. "Janine, tell me your favorite thing you remember about Dad."

"When I was little, I remember he'd count to three and throw me up to the sky. I used to love that." Janine laughed.

"He used to do that to me when I was little too."

"Mom never did that kind of stuff."

"Naw. That was a Daddy thing." I said. Now Janine had turned around and stretched out my pocket by pressing her feet against my chest and her head against the inside of the pocket fabric. She looked like the center pole holding up a tent. She seemed lonely.

"Mom's too busy trying to keep up with us. Think about it. She used to be fun."

"Oh. I guess you're right." Janine was quiet. She probably missed Mom and Dad too.

"Is that comfortable?"

"Yeah, it is. Your pocket keeps pushing my head back in while you walk, then I push out with my feet. It's like being inside a pogo stick, I think. Anyway, the clouds are neat to look at."

"You know, I used to hike in the mountains with Dad," I said. "I think he knew the names of every tree and grass and flower there was."

"Yeah. I remember when he'd take me down to the lake, he'd show me all the different birds and try to get me to learn their names," Janine said. "I wasn't any good at remembering them."

"Janine, how come you think Dad knew so much?" I asked.

"I don't know. Maybe it was all stuff he had to learn to work for Madame G."

I hadn't thought of that. He probably did know all that stuff to help him out on his missions. I didn't know a fraction of what he did. If someone with his knowledge and training could get caught up and lost on a mission, how in the world was I going to succeed? I saw a tiny movement out of the corner of my eye. As I scanned the trail, I realized the gnome sentries were all around us. It wouldn't do to tell this to Janine, so I tried to remain calm. Their sinister stares gave me the goose bumps, though.

"Robert! Duck!" Janine's yell roused me from my thoughts.

I dropped to the ground and covered my head as a shadow passed over. Then I heard Janine laughing hysterically from the depths of my pocket, where she'd tumbled.

"It's a duck. Look over there."

I turned to see a flock of ducks flying low overhead. They landed in a small pond to our left. "Very funny, Janine."

"Well, you fell for it," she said, popping her head back out, giggling. I walked on with my mouth clamped tight. I hated when Janine got the best of me. Eventually, she stopped laughing, and we continued in silence for a while.

"Robert, look at the rock. It's got eyes," Janine squeaked.

"That's not a rock, Janine." I whispered. "I think that's one of the gnome men Delfini told me about."

"It looks like an ugly rock to me."

"Shh. He might hear you." For once, I was grateful for Janine's irritatingly high-pitched voice. I didn't really know, but it seemed to me that the gnome men, with their ears made of rock, would have trouble with a voice like Janine's. I hoped it came through like a mosquito buzzing. "Look carefully and you'll see some more of them. I started noticing them right before the pond."

I directed Janine's attention to the rocks rising out of the earth on either side of the path. Most of them looked like, well, like rocks. But every so often, if you watched carefully, a pair of eyes stared right back at you from inside the rock. I assumed that these weren't rocks at all, but the mountain gnome sentries camouflaging themselves. Their vague outlines were almost invisible. I hoped the book was right about them leaving us alone. I could not afford to waste all my cheese just trying to get past them.

Janine resumed her hammock position in my pocket, staring up at the sky. "Robert, look!" She pointed over my shoulder.

"Oh, no. I'm not falling for that again." I laughed at her. "Fool me once, shame on you. Fool me twice, shame on me."

"No, Robert. Duck now!" Janine screamed as loudly as she could. At that moment, rough pincers grabbed the back of my shirt.

"Hey, what's going on?" Something lifted me off the ground. My feet flapped helplessly as I tried to get a look at what had me. It had scaly brown bird feet.

"Robert, it's some kind of bird monster!" Janine stared wide-eyed at my unknown assailant.

"Janine, get back in your house, now!" I didn't have to tell her twice. We rose higher as the bird carried us toward the top of the mountain. Finally, it dropped us into its huge nest on the edge of a cliff near the volcano's crater.

The empty nest looked about twice as wide as I was tall, around eleven feet in diameter, and made of logs covered in grey moss. The bird circled the nest after dropping us. Immediately, I dug into my pack, looking for some more Muenster. I figured this bird thing qualified under the "many monsters" part of the second secret.

As the giant bird approached the nest, I cocked my arm back, ready to unload the Muenster. The bird rocked the nest slightly as it alighted on the end opposite me. Immediately, I threw the cheese at it. With one swift motion, it snapped it up in its huge beak and dropped it into the nest.

"Excellent throw, Robert," the bird spoke out in a melodic voice, "but you shouldn't waste your valuable Muenster on me."

I stared, open-mouthed at the bird. It was about ten feet tall, with shimmering golden feathers. Its face was not a bird's face at all. It was a woman's face, except for the beak. A silvery glow came from its eyes and it reminded me of my mom. I knew instantly that it meant me no harm.

"I am Pouli, the mother of all birds. I am a simurgh. Madame Gorgonzola sent me to help you."

"You know Madame Gorgonzola?" I asked, dumbfounded.

"Yes, I am a friend of the Syndicate. She watches your

progress and your time is running short."

"Can you take us to the city of Eliki then? I didn't like the looks of those gnome sentries on the mountain."

"No, I cannot, Robert, but I can shorten your journey to the crater's mouth. There a son of Gob must help you."

"Here." Pouli pushed a shiny gold berry toward me. "Eat this. It will give you wisdom for the remainder of your journey."

"Oooh. Can I have one?" Janine interrupted for the umpteenth time.

"Little Janine. I believe you need only a drop of juice from the Gnosi Berry. Robert, please share with Janine."

Irritated, I glared at Janine while I held the berry out and squeezed a drop into her open mouth. She looked like a baby bird gulping it down. I supposed that was fitting in a bird's nest. I popped the berry into my mouth. Its honey sweetness melted much too quickly across my tongue.

"Man, that was better than Madame G.'s elixir," Janine announced.

Pouli chuckled a beautiful harmonic laugh. "Come, children. You shall ride on my wing for the rest of the journey. I trust it will be better than dangling from my claws. Robert, put that Muenster back into your pack. We must be off."

84

I climbed onto Pouli's wing and sank into her feathers. As we flew, she sang a beautiful wordless melody. Soon I was dreaming. It was the strangest dream I'd ever had.

My dad was there. So were Madame G., Stefano, Pouli, and a bunch of other weird characters I didn't know. It looked like some sort of council meeting. Everyone sat in a circle arguing. Finally, it looked like they came to an agreement because my father stood up. Some big, burly guards led in some sort of monster in chains. I knew that monster. It was the chimera. Now I could see that the middle head was a goat. It looked even more disgusting in my dream than in the forest last night.

My father read something to the chimera from a scroll he was holding. The different members of the council nodded their heads in agreement. The chimera looked angrier every second. My father finished speaking and the guards started to lead the chimera away. They had to drag the monster because it pulled against the chains, shaking its heads violently.

Now the scene changed. The guards were trying to get the chimera into a prison cell. It looked like they were in some kind of dungeon. The monster was resisting with full force. All of a sudden, its three heads attacked the guards, killing them instantly. It bounded up the dungeon steps.

That was the last part of the dream. I awoke to Pouli's whisper entreating me to get up.

"Robert, we are at the entrance to the bowels of the earth. I must leave you here, as I cannot live under rock. I hope my lullaby and the Gnosi berry will serve you well."

I climbed down and stood facing Pouli. "Pouli, I had this strange dream."

She stopped me by gently placing her claw on my foot. "That was my gift to you," she said. "I looked into your mind and provided you with one answer you were looking for. I can answer only one question in your dreams. I hope I chose a good one for you." She stared at me with those beautiful eyes.

"So that's why the chimera hates me so much?" I said, more to myself than to her. "My father sentenced it to the dungeon."

"Your father captured it for the Syndicate. The elders sentenced it to imprisonment," Pouli corrected me. "It had done a great many evils. Unfortunately, it escaped."

"Why didn't you just kill it?"

"Robert, to sentence a creature to death is a very grave matter. We had hopes that the chimera could be reformed. It was once a member of the Syndicate."

"That thing was on our side?" I asked, not believing.

"Do not be fooled by appearances, Robert. Many things that seem foul may indeed be fair. Come now, you must be on your way." Pouli turned her head toward the crater.

"Well, good-bye," I said, "and thanks."

"It has been my pleasure, Robert. Good luck." Pouli took flight, leaving the breeze from her wings as a final token of her aid.

Chapter 9

Into the Bowels
of the Earth

After Pouli's departure, I surveyed the landscape inside the crater. Dark, ancient formations rose around every side of us. We stood on a black lava dome. I couldn't see any obvious caves or trails, so I decided it was time to call for the gnomes.

"Sons of Gob, I need your assistance." I froze as the rocks began to move toward me. I should have expected it, I suppose, after seeing the sentries on the trail, but the sight of these short, grotesque men emerging from the rocks gave me chills. Their faces, arms, and legs seemed to be made of stone. Pebbly warts covered their fingers. Long, grey-green beards hung from their chins. The beards reminded me of the lichens that grow on trees and rocks. Atop their heads, each wore a dull, mud-colored, pointed cap. They circled me slowly and formed a tight ring.

"They sure are ugly," Janine whispered from my pocket.

"Shh! The book said not to mention their appearance."

"Oh, yeah, I forgot. I'm going inside. You can deal with them." She disappeared into my pocket, and I heard the door click shut. At least I wouldn't have to worry about Janine saying something she shouldn't.

Turning my attention to the gnomes, I called out, "I am Robert Montasio, of the Secret Cheese Syndicate. I require a guide through your realm to the ancient city of Eliki." Not too bad, I thought. I was finally starting to sound like a real agent.

A stocky gnome stepped forward. "Syndicate Agent, I am Mikrainos, leader of the sons of Gob. We care neither for you nor your quest, but we will honor your right to passage if you provide proper payment. What have you to offer us?"

I thought about what I'd already used up: half a wheel of Cheddar and one wheel of Muenster. I had better not give any more of those away. I'd have to wing it and hope I didn't give him something I would really need later. "I offer you two wheels of cheese."

The ring of gnomes stomped their stone feet in unison, shaking the entire crater. It sounded worse than the time I went to a pro football game and the crowd started pounding their aluminum seats because they didn't like the referee's call.

"More! More!" The gnomes shouted with deafening cries while my legs shook from the stomping.

"Mikrainos," I spoke directly to the leader, trying to keep my own voice from shaking. "I can offer two wheels of cheese, no more. What is your answer?"

The gnome mob quieted to a murmur as he raised his hand to speak. "My comrades, you can see, are very demanding. Two wheels of cheese for safe passage through our kingdom? The journey is long and treacherous. You insult me, Agent of Cheese." He folded his arms and turned his head. At that, they took up the chant, louder than before.

"Name your price then, gnome," I shouted to Mikrainos over the din. I didn't know why I said that, but after the words came out, I figured it would be good to see how greedy this guy actually was.

Mikrainos motioned for silence. Immediately, the wild voices ceased. "Agent of Cheese, I do not ask for much. Merely one half of a wheel of cheese for each sentinel who accompanies you." He stepped back and waited for my answer.

It seemed reasonable. Half a wheel of cheese wasn't that much. I was about to agree when Janine, who'd obviously been eavesdropping again from inside the dollhouse, whispered, "Look at all those guys. That'll take up all of our cheese and then some."

I glanced down, but couldn't see her. "What do you think I should do?" I whispered back.

"I don't know. You'd better make sure he doesn't try to bring everyone. He looks like a con man to me."

"What say you, Agent of Cheese?" Mikrainos asked with his foot tapping.

I looked straight into his cold, stony eyes. "Mikrainos, I shall agree to your price on one condition. I choose the guides." I smiled. That was a pretty good idea, I thought.

"Done." Mikrainos sneered. His lipless grin mocked me at the close of the deal.

I pursed my lips, hoping my plan would work. "I choose you, Mikrainos. You are the only guide I will need."

"Treachery!" Mikrainos roared as he reached out his arms. I cringed, thinking he was going to attack me right there. "The passage through stone is most treacherous. You cannot choose only one guide," Mikrainos said through clenched teeth. The ring of gnomes shuddered with disapproval and murmured to each other.

"You agreed to my conditions, Mikrainos. Are you a man of your word?" I shouted back, gaining confidence. Somewhere, inside my head, I knew I was doing the right thing. I waited patiently while Mikrainos paced and fumed. He knew he could not take back the agreement. I had him beat. Finally, he spoke.

"Come, Agent of Cheese." Mikrainos shook his head in defeat. "This will be a very difficult journey without my brothers."

"Quick thinking, Robert," Janine piped up again as we followed Mikrainos into the shadows. "You've gotten a lot smarter since we started this trip."

"I've always been this smart. You just never noticed."

"Yeah, right," she snorted in her old Janine way. "Must have been Pouli's Gnosi Berry."

"You're probably right." I laughed. Janine didn't seem as irritating as usual. "You know, Janine, I think you might just be growing up a little."

"You think?"

"Agent who speaks to empty space," Mikrainos interjected. Obviously, he couldn't see or hear Janine. "We are entering the passages under the earth."

"It's awfully dark in here. Can we have a light?"

"Silence!" He turned to me and hissed. "Do not waken the spirits of the rock. They do not take kindly to abovegrounders. You have foolishly chosen to undertake this journey with only myself as protection. I shall fulfill my oath, but you must obey my commands. Otherwise, I cannot guarantee your safe passage."

I thought he had just been angry about my tricking him. Maybe I should have chosen a few more guides. At half a cheese apiece, I could have gotten four guides for my original offer of two wheels of cheese. It was too late to backtrack now. Something in Mikrainos' voice made me think he'd be glad if we got into some sort of trouble.

"Place your hand on my shoulder," he commanded. "From this point forward, you need to maintain physical contact with me. Otherwise, you will be lost inside the earth."

I did as he asked without comment. He was as tall as Janine used to be, so my hand rested easily on his shoulder. The black walls of the crater had long since narrowed to a small corridor-like pathway. I could barely make out Mikrainos' cap outline in front of my face, and the light was fading fast. Soon we were in complete darkness.

I don't know how it happened, but after walking for some time into the shrinking crevice, the path completely vanished. The space around me disappeared, but I continued to move. Dirt, pebbles, and rock flowed past me as my feet dangled. I wasn't walking at all. It was as though Mikrainos swam through the rock, and I dragged behind in his wake. I gripped his shoulder tightly as my feet swung freely behind me. Dirt and stone flowed past my arms and legs. The constant backflow of earth behind me was suffocating. I had dirt in my nostrils, and I wanted terribly to scratch my eyes to get the dust out, but I didn't dare let go of Mikrainos' shoulder. I could no longer see anything. I felt like I was drowning in dirt.

The earth around me pressed in harder as we descended farther. I felt pinches and grabs from unknown assailants, and large boulders refused to move, jabbing me whenever they could. At some point, something yanked me and pulled on my backpack. I felt it slipping, but I couldn't let go of Mikrainos' shoulder, or I'd be lost for sure. I kept my mouth shut and hoped Janine didn't decide to chime in until we got through this mess.

Maybe I was hallucinating, but I could swear I heard voices. They weren't very nice, either. Whatever else Mikrainos was, he was right about the earth not liking me. My tiny air bubble got smaller and smaller. Even though it was pitch black, I panicked when I had to shut my eyes because the open space behind Mikrainos had shrunk to include only my nose and mouth. A few more feet and I would have no breathing room at all.

Finally, the last pocket of air collapsed and dirt rushed

into my nose and mouth. I knew that this was the end. I'd failed Madame Gorgonzola, my dad, even Janine. My lungs pressed in on me, just like when I stayed under water too long. I figured I'd lose consciousness in about ninety seconds.

I suddenly started choking and coughing. The choking turned to sputtering as I spit out rock and dirt. I realized I was standing up. My eyes opened, and I saw that earth no longer surrounded me. A faint light, like that from a campfire, glowed somewhere in the distance. Clean air rushed into my lungs after I coughed out the last pebble. I looked over to see Mikrainos standing, smug-faced, with his arm outstretched.

"How?" I coughed again. "How'd you do that?" I asked him.

"I will take my payment now, Agent of Cheese." Mikrainos wiggled his open palm.

"But I couldn't breathe. How?"

"My payment. I am waiting." Mikrainos tapped the palm of his outstretched hand with a finger from the other hand. He stared off into the distance, studying something on the cave ceiling. He refused to look at me.

I could see I wasn't going to get an answer from him. And I did owe him my life. I didn't like the idea of being in debt to such an awful little creature. I reached around my shoulder to get my pack. My stomach leaped into my mouth. It was gone.

"Mikrainos! My pack is gone! Something pulled it off my back while we were going through the rock."

"Agent of Cheese," Mikrainos said as he took a step towards me. "We have an agreement. You MUST make payment, or your life is forfeit to me!"

"But I …" I backed up until I hit the wall of the cavern.

"I warned you, Agent of Cheese." Mikrainos continued approaching, his fists clenched into tight balls. "You should have listened to me. We needed more guides for a safe journey. You shall pay for this mistake."

The cave wall began erupting all around me as more sons of Gob popped out, each spraying the floor with a shower of pebbles. Soon a ring of gnomes surrounded me on three sides. I closed my eyes as their cold, hard hands grabbed me. I felt sweat pouring from my hot face. I had no idea what they planned to do to me, but I hoped they'd get it over with quickly.

"Sons of Gob! Desist!" I knew that voice. It was Skylos. I let out a long sigh. How did he get here? I didn't know, and I didn't care. Even though Skylos didn't like me, he was on my side.

Relief rushed into every one of my limbs.

"Skylos!" Mikrainos turned to challenge my rescuer. "You will not save him. He has no payment. Therefore, he belongs to me."

"I have his payment." Skylos, his teeth bared, approached Mikrainos. "You must accept it." He growled.

"No!" shouted Mikrainos. "I will not accept it. He could not fulfill the contract. He must pay the consequences."

In a flash, Skylos jumped Mikrainos, knocking him flat. He stood with his paws on Mikrainos' chest. I watched the fear in the gnome man's eyes as Skylos bent close to his face and growled. "You will take payment, or you will deal with me!" Skylos looked up and addressed the other gnomes. "ALL of you will deal with me!"

Without warning, the gnomes let go of me. They squealed and backed away, each trying to use the others as a shield. It looked like a pack of rats climbing over each other to escape a flood. Then, one by one, they reentered the rock. In a moment, they were all gone.

Mikrainos glanced with fear from Skylos to me. His army had deserted him. "I will accept payment," he grumbled.

"I knew you would see it my way," Skylos said as he

stepped off Mikrainos' chest. "Robert, come and retrieve your things," Skylos said to me in a kinder voice than usual. I walked over to him and took my pack from his back. "Please pay this miserable gnome."

I unzipped my pack and dumped the contents, and a great deal of dirt, onto the cavern floor. My knees went weak, all of a sudden, and I leaned against a large boulder and waved my hand over the pile. "You may have your choice, Mikrainos." I didn't have the energy to rummage through anything. I just wanted Mikrainos to go.

He picked through the pile. Spying a wheel of bright orange cheese I did not recognize, his expression changed. He barely contained himself as he said, "I will take the Vieux Boulogne. It is a great delicacy." As he began to cut it in half, I doubled over from the awful aroma. It was worse than Madame G. when I first met her.

Janine came screaming out of her house. "What is that nasty smell? Robert, we must be in a sewage plant!" She stopped short to see Mikrainos inhaling the waves of odiferous vapor. "He can't really like that, can he?" She looked up at me holding her nose.

"Who can know the mysterious mind of a gnome?" I gave a halfhearted laugh. Mystical or not, that cheese needed to go before we all collapsed under its noxious fumes.

"Stop, Mikrainos." I pointed to the cheese. "Take the whole thing."

He looked at me in astonishment. "You give away the stinkiest cheese in the world? You are more foolish than I thought." Cackling, he dove back into the cavern wall with the cheese in tow.

"Thanks for all your help!" I called after him. He probably didn't hear me, as his feet disappeared into the rock with a final kick before I finished speaking. I know he didn't like me any better than the ground did.

I don't know why I bothered thanking him anyway, seeing as he was going to beat me up, or worse, before Skylos arrived. Skylos! I turned around to see him stretched out on the ground, panting. He looked tired.

"Skylos. You saved my life. I don't know how to repay you."

"You cannot," he said. Well, that was blunt, wasn't it? "Robert. It is not your fault that you lost your pack this time," he continued in a softer voice. "The underworld is no place for a child." He shook his head and muttered, "I counseled against it."

"What do you mean, you counseled against it?" I asked him.

"Robert, I voted against sending you on this quest. I

99

thought you too young."

Here we go again. Another, "you're not capable" lecture. I kicked a rock and looked away with disgust. Tears welled up in my eyes, but I was determined not to let Skylos see them. He'd take it as another sign of weakness.

"Do not misunderstand me, Robert." Skylos cocked his head knowingly to one side. "You will make a fine agent, one day. However, I fear the danger of this journey is too much for you. It matters not. You must now finish what you have begun."

I looked back to him. So, he didn't think I was a complete idiot. That was hopeful, at least. "Yeah, but with you bailing me out every time, how can I go wrong?" I gave him a little smile.

"Robert," Skylos gave a great doggie sigh. "I cannot help you again."

"What do you mean? You've done it three times already."

"My number is three," Skylos explained. "I may offer assistance thrice on any mission. I have no power to help you again until you end the quest."

"What?" I asked as my heart sank. "You mean, I'm on my own now?" I always thought I was on my own, but looking back, I realized I'd been helped out by a whole slew of the good guys.

"You are on your own," Skylos said resting his muzzle on his paws.

"Nobody else can help me?"

"Robert. You have your mind. It is keener than I believed at my first observation. And do not forget that you have Janine," he reminded me.

Janine. She was irritating, but I had to give her credit. Some of her advice hadn't been half bad. We'd come a long way together since yesterday. My hopes began to rise.

"Robert," Skylos said, "you don't have much farther to go now. The city of Eliki is a short distance from here. I believe you will finish well. You are your father's son."

"You knew my father?" I asked.

"Marco Montasio is a great friend of mine. I pray you find him, for all our sakes."

I choked up. "I will," I whispered.

Skylos rose and shook. A great cloud of dust escaped from his matted, tangled fur. "Robert Montasio, I bid you adieu." With that, Skylos turned and trotted off into the darkness.

"Good-bye, Skylos," I said softly, waving my hand. Alone again, I sat down and looked around. We were in a huge underground cavern. Pale orange light came from somewhere. In the distance, ancient buildings glowed in an eerie tint.

Janine popped up to check out the scene. "So this is Eliki," she commented. "It's about time we got here." The fragrance of the Vieux Boulogne hung faintly in the air.

"I'm just glad we can breathe," I answered, stuffing the backpack again.

"Robert," she said. "You did a good job with that Mikrainos character."

I looked at her to see if she was teasing me. It was hard to tell in the cave light.

"I'm serious. But I'm sure glad Skylos showed up when he did."

"You and me both," I replied.

"How do you think he does that, anyway?"

"Does what?"

"You know. Shows up to save our butts." She laughed.

"I have no idea. But did you hear what he told me?" I looked at her.

"Yeah. He won't be coming back. That's kind of scary."

"I'm not going to think about that. I'd rather concentrate on the other stuff he said."

"Like what?" she asked.

"Well, first he said we're almost done. Then he said we made a good team."

"We do, don't we?" Janine giggled.

"What's so funny?" I asked.

"Well, if you must know, Delfini told me I needed to start helping you out. You know, stop giving you so much grief. SHE said we'd never make it to the end if we were fighting all the time. So, hard as it is, I'm trying to keep my mouth shut when we're in a big jam."

Standing up, I stretched before putting on the pack. "Thanks, sis. I think you're doing okay."

"High praise indeed," she said. "I'm beginning to sound like a Syndicate member." She bent over laughing. "Maybe they'll induct me when we get back."

"Come on, we're not there yet," I said and started down the road to the city.

Chapter 10

The Lost City

I looked at the paving stones that formed the ancient road to Eliki. Maybe this had once been a great highway, but now it was pitted with holes and cracks. Huge sections of road were missing, probably sunk during the earthquake that buried the city.

I picked my way carefully among the rubble, occasionally glancing into the deep abyss. A fiery glow shone up through some of the holes. Apparently, this volcano wasn't completely dead. That explained the light.

As I made slow and steady progress, the crumbling watchtowers of the city's gate loomed closer. To my left the road gave way to a field of boulders. I imagined how the field must have looked when the city was above the ground: probably green with trees, grass, and wildflowers.

On the right side of the road, a dark, silent lake filled the cavern. I didn't know how big it was, but it seemed to continue past the last shadow cast by the dim light. I tried not to think about what might live under its surface, but goosebumps tingled up my arms, making me shudder.

As I approached the crumbling gate, it occurred to me that the city might be inhabited. It looked deserted, but I decided to be as careful as I could. Keeping to the shadows, I tried to approach unseen even though there appeared to be no one at the gate.

Inside, the city was like a maze. The stone walls, although cracked, were high, and the lane narrow. Ahead of me, the passage divided into three paths. I stopped before walking three feet, realizing I would soon be lost if I didn't come up with a plan. I remembered Stefano's maps and took them out, carefully unrolling them.

"I wish I had a light," I grumbled, thinking about Stefano's poor planning. Instantly the outline and writing on the maps began to glow.

"Robert, that is too cool!" Janine said.

"Yeah, I wonder what else I can just wish for."

I rerolled the first map, which was pretty much a standard map of Europe, and tucked it back into my pack. The second map showed how to navigate the maze of streets inside Eliki. Where had Stefano gotten a map like this? It didn't really matter. I was glad to have it. Poseidon's statue was at the city's center. To reach it, I needed to take the middle fork each time the road split. That was easy enough. Supposedly, the treasure chamber lay somewhere in his trident. Words blazed on the map, just above the statue: *Beware the Chamber Guard.*

"Humph," Janine whispered, "you knew it wasn't going to be too easy."

"Aw, c'mon, Janine," I bragged, "I am Robert Montasio, after all. How much trouble can one little guard be?" I hoped she couldn't see how scared I really was.

"Aided by your incredibly talented and resourceful little sister?" she added. "No trouble at all."

I wondered how afraid Janine was, but I wasn't about to ask. While I walked past each split in the path, I wondered about the guard. The only picture that formed in my mind was that of the manticore. I hoped the guard didn't turn out to be one of those.

The path widened to a large circular space after the fifth passage split. Amid the crumpled buildings, at the very center of the round plaza, stood an immense statue of Poseidon. It was probably fifty feet tall and looked like it was made of gold. Poseidon stared defiantly, trident in hand. His crowned head bore a striking resemblance to Triton.

I crept from stone to stone, not wanting the guard to see me. With each short scoot, I looked for a guard but didn't see one. Finally, when I was within twenty feet of the statue's base, I spotted it, sleeping.

"I thought the gnomes were ugly," Janine whispered, "but that thing is beyond ugly."

Janine was right. The guard's glittery green skin glowed in the soft light. She—at least I thought it was a she—was about five feet tall. She leaned against the base of the trident, eyes closed. Her long arms ended in bony fingers. From the tips of her fingers protruded sharp red fingernails. The scariest-looking part of her, however, was her head. It was covered in hundreds of tiny snakes. They seemed to be sleeping too.

"Robert, you'd better find out what that is," Janine advised.

"Good idea," I agreed.

I hid behind a half-destroyed wall and took out my field guide. I looked in the index for snakes. There were chapters on adders, basilisks, and cobras. None of those were helpful. I looked for snake women, nothing.

Flipping back to the table of contents, I scanned the headings. At the bottom of the page was a chapter entitled "Unknown Creature Identification." I turned to page 89 and began to read.

This chapter read like a scientific key. The first line had

two choices: human-like or animal-like. Was this guard a human or an animal? It looked like a woman, but had all those snakes in her hair. I decided human. The key said go to choice number 25. I did that: man or woman. That one was easy enough. Woman, go to choice 50.

This process went on for about ten more choices, each asking questions about the creature's appearance. There were even sketches to help me identify certain features. When I got to choice 87, I stopped and stared at the pictures, then read the description under the one that matched.

> *This creature is a Gorgon. There were three original Gorgons who were children of the sea gods. Medusa, the most famous, was killed by Perseus. If you stared at her head, you would have turned to stone. Her sisters, Stheno and Euryale, cannot turn you to stone, but their blood is poison. The Gorgonzola cheese family is distantly related to the Gorgons, but that fact is not widely publicized.*

I slammed the book shut and looked at Janine. "What should we do now?" I asked, hoping she had a good suggestion.

"What do you mean, 'we'?" she said. "It's your job to get the cheese."

"Come on, Janine," I whined. "You love telling me what to do. Now's your chance. The book doesn't give any advice."

"You got any idea how Perseus killed that one called Medusa?" Janine asked after thinking for a moment.

"By the looks of this picture, I'd say he cut off her head," I said after looking back at the book. "But I don't have a sword, and I'm not sure I could do that, even if she tried to attack us."

"Beats me," Janine said. "Well, whatever you do, don't let her get any blood on you. Then you'll croak, and I'll never get out of here."

"Thanks a lot, Janine. That was really helpful."

I emptied my sack, hoping to find some inspiration for dealing with the sleeping Gorgon. The only thing that caught my eye was the empty notebook Stefano had packed. Flubbed again! I'd forgotten to take notes. Better late than never.

I opened the book and started thinking about my day. As the thoughts formed in my mind, they appeared on the page. I was telepathically writing. I wondered if Stefano would let me keep this notebook for school. Probably not, but maybe I'd conveniently forget to give it back. I continued committing the day to words.

Chapter 11

The Gorgon Takes
the Cheese

"Well, well, well. What have we here?" A cackling voice floated down from the ledge above me. I looked up from my magical notebook to see the grotesque face of the Gorgon, all one hundred plus of her snake hairs hissing at me. Quickly, I jumped up and backed away from the wall. She leapt down from the rock, prancing and skipping around me.

"I am Robert Montasio." I left out the part about the Cheese Syndicate.

"Are you another of those Syndicate punks?" She gave me a bored expression as she flicked dust from her gown. The pale, silvery dress hung limply around her skinny body, reflecting the green light. I think it had once been something like you'd see Cinderella wear to a ball, but it was tattered and worn.

"Another one?" I asked stupidly.

"Yeah. Some guy came through awhile back. He was

pretty sharp, if I remember correctly."

I wondered if she was talking about my father. Maybe he had been here. "How long ago?"

"Who knows? It's so hard to keep track of time down in this forsaken place. No sunlight, you know. It does terrible things to my beautiful skin." She patted her green face so gingerly I almost laughed. The snakes let out a collective moan.

"Was his name Marco Montasio?"

"Could have been."

I didn't know how much to tell this creature. She was probably one of the bad guys, after all, but she didn't look like she was too interested in hurting me.

"Where is he now?"

"You sure are full of questions. Look, I'm not the library information service. If you want more details you're going to have to come up with something for me."

She wanted me to pay her to tell me about my dad. I dug in my pockets. "I've got five bucks," I said, holding out a Lincoln.

"Paper? What am I going to do with paper?" Her snake braids all rolled their eyes in unison with her.

"What do you want?" I asked and threw up my hands.

"Got any cheese?"

Another cheese bargain. The book should have said something about this. I thought about throwing my Muenster at her, but somehow, I don't think it would have the same effect on her as on the ozaena. She seemed less like a monster and more like an evil villain. I knew there was more Cheddar than anything else in the pack.

"I've got some Cheddar to trade."

"Cheddar?" She laughed and all the snakeheads hissed. "How mundane. Don't they teach you anything in your famous Syndicate School?"

"Sorry, I didn't really get a chance to go to the school." I shuffled my feet. "Hey, wait a minute." I glared at her. "How do you know so much about the Syndicate?"

"Madame G. must be really hard up these days, sending out rookies like you." She sniffed, rather impolitely. "Look buddy, how I know what I know is my own business. You got any good stuff for me, or should I eat you right here and now?"

"What do you want?" I held out my hands, hoping she didn't see the sweat on my palms. I sure wished Skylos could show up again. He'd know what to do.

"I'm a hairy brute, get it? Okay, my lovely locks are a little exotic." She stopped here to pat the snakeheads, while they flicked their tongues onto her fingers. It was disgusting. "But they count as hair," she said.

"You mean those snakes in your head?"

"Duh. Yes, they're my hair."

"So you want the Port Salut? But won't it kill you or something?"

"Ah!" She screamed in frustration. "Port Salut rids you of the hairy brute! Just give me some of the cheese, or I will eat you this instant."

"You like Port Salut?" I'd never considered that something as evil looking as this character would like the mystical cheeses.

"Like it? I love it. I live for it. But I don't get much of it down here in this dreary place. Stheno got the cushy job guarding the temple of Zeus, while I'm stuck here in the dungeon." She paced back and forth, raising her hands. "How many more years will I be stuck in this job?"

I could tell she wasn't talking to me anymore. "So you're Euryale," I stated.

"Yeah, that's my name."

"How'd you get this nasty assignment anyway?" I thought I'd press my luck. She liked to talk, and I figured the longer we chatted, the more time I'd have to get out of this mess, and the less likely it would be that I'd end up as her snakes' breakfast.

"Well, it wasn't my fault, you know." She turned, flashing her luminescent topaz eyes at me. "I got fired from my position as guardian at the Oracle of Didyma. I was supposed to intercept someone, but I was tricked. Now I'm here." She collapsed on a low stone, obviously deflated.

"That's too bad." I tried to sound sympathetic.

"Hey, Euryale." Janine picked this moment to pop her head out. "Don't feel so bad."

"Janine, be quiet," I spat.

"Oh, what is this?" Euryale came closer to get a good look at Janine. She was even scarier-looking up close, and she stunk like my lucky basketball socks. I backed up.

"I'm Janine, Robert's little sister."

I moaned. I wished she would shut up.

"You know," Janine continued, ignoring my stares. "Robert messed up his first assignment with the Syndicate."

"How cute," Euryale laughed, "a mini-sized Syndicate punk. What will Gi-Gi think of next?"

"Who's Gi-Gi?" Janine asked.

"My rotten, do-good cousin."

"You mean Gi-Gi is Madame Gorgonzola?" I asked her.

"Yeah. She's the one who got me into trouble in the first place. When she outsmarted me at the Oracle, I got banished." Euryale turned her attention back to Janine. "So give me the scoop on Robert."

I grimaced as Janine proceeded to recount how she shrunk.

"Well, Robert," Euryale said, "looks like you and I aren't so different after all."

"There is one difference between us, Euryale," I said.

"Yeah, what's that?"

"I've got the cheese, and you don't."

She huffed and puffed and then sank to the ground. She seemed so pathetic I almost felt sorry for her. "Okay, Euryale. I'll give it to you on one condition," I said.

She looked up with a renewed glint in her eye. "You, boy, are not in the position to impose conditions." She breathed on her long, sharp fingernails and rubbed them against the silky part of her dress.

I decided right there not to ever feel sorry for her. Negotiation was what I needed. "But I'll give you two wheels of it." I smiled.

She looked greedily at the pack. "Okay, what's your condition?"

"You have to tell me what happened to Marco Montasio

when he was down here."

"No problem, boy. Give me the cheese."

I reached into the sack and pulled out two wheels of cheese. I handed her one. She tore off the wrapping and sunk her spiny sharp teeth into it. The Port Salut was history in about ten seconds as she snorted and gulped her way through it.

"She eats like a pig," I whispered.

"You ought to know." Janine giggled.

"Aw, shut up."

Only after she'd consumed the last crumb and licked the packaging did she look up.

"What about my other wheel?" She stared at the other cheese I held in my hand.

"First tell me about Marco."

"Oh, all right." She stuck out her lower lip, eyeing the other piece of Port Salut. "He paid the entrance fee and entered the chamber. I got tired of waiting for him to come out. He probably slipped by while I was taking a nap."

"That's it?" I asked, incredulous.

"What else do you want from me?" She held her hand out. "Now give me the rest of the cheese, and you get one hour of peace."

I looked at her. "What do you mean, 'one hour of peace'"?"

"Don't you read anything in that useless manual of yours?"

I grinned. "I'm a little behind on my reading."

She sighed, along with all her snake buddies. "The Port Salut rids you of the hairy brute for one hour. After that you are fair game, and I'll come after you if you're still here."

"You wouldn't really eat me, would you, Euryale?" I teased her. "I'm not very tasty."

"Try me," she said, smacking her lips.

I thought about those teeth and how quickly they had dispatched the cheese. "Wait a minute. Don't I get two hours since you got two wheels of cheese?"

"No way, buddy. One hour each time you strike a deal." She bared her teeth at me. "You got a problem with that?"

"No. I guess not," I said. I'd hoped to squeeze a little more time out of her. "Okay, when does my hour start?"

She reached behind her head and pulled out a tiny hourglass from her hair. Her snake friends must keep it in place back there. "I'll flip this as soon as you hand me the cheese, and that's being generous. The guidelines say I could have started the timer when I got the first hunk."

"Gee, thanks, Euryale." I flashed a smile, tossed the cheese to her, and raced toward the statue.

"Toodle-lou," Euryale called out. "The door's in his big toe."

Chapter 12

The Poseidon Adventure

"Run, Robert. Run!" Janine yelled from inside my pocket. I was running as fast as I could but didn't take the time to tell her that. The statue looked like it was two football fields away. We reached the foot of the statue in about one minute. I'm a good sprinter.

Poseidon's big toe was about seven feet tall, at least. Looking past his foot I followed the statue up to the trident, which he held in the opposite hand. It seemed about five hundred feet in the air.

"How are we going to get to the trident if we have to enter at his foot?" Janine wondered.

"Let's worry about getting in first," I panted. Tracing my fingers along the outline of a smooth, handle-less door, I could find no hinges. "How am I supposed to open it?" I asked myself aloud.

"Why don't you just push on it?" Janine stated the obvious again.

I shook my head. Why could I not think of these

things myself? I gave the door a push, and it silently swung inward. "Cool. Quality workmanship."

"What are you talking about?" Janine asked.

"Mr. Jaworski, my shop teacher, always harps about 'quality workmanship.' He says if you build something right, it will work forever. I think this is what he's talking about."

"Not like that bookshelf you made for Mom." Janine laughed. "It collapsed when she put a magazine on it."

I smiled, remembering the Mother's Day gift. "Yeah. Not my best moment."

We entered Poseidon's foot and found a long antechamber scattered with a few tables and chairs, probably a guardroom in the old days. Torches lined the wall every twenty feet or so. After the third torch, the room ended with a stairway.

"That's how we get up to the trident." I pointed to the stairs.

"It's going to be a long climb. Call me when we get there," Janine disappeared into my pocket.

Once again, I was left with all the hard work. I'd climbed ten flights of stairs when I found an open window. Looking out, I guessed I was at Poseidon's knee. I could see Euryale at her station in the distance. She looked bored. Maybe she'd forgotten about eating me. Just as that thought popped into my head, I saw her reach for something. It was too far away to see, but I bet it was the hourglass. I continued the climb.

After another twelve flights, the stairway widened into a great room with a huge cathedral ceiling, lost somewhere in the dark space above me. The stairwell continued going up near the wall, but I walked out to examine the room.

It, too, was empty, except for long rows of shelves. They lined the walls and precisely crossed the center of the room. A few books littered the floor, and fragments of broken pottery and statues were strewn about. Apparently, someone, or many someones, had cleaned this place out over the years. Turning to get back to the stairs, I heard Janine's voice.

"Robert, don't we need to get to the trident?"

"Yeah, that's where the cheese is supposed to be," I said, looking down at her tiny head scanning the room.

"Don't you think you should try the other stairs then?" she asked me.

"What other stairs?"

"Well, we came up his left leg, right?"

I nodded.

"Isn't the trident in his right hand?" she said, a little too self-satisfied.

I hate it when she's right. I turned around again and headed toward the other side of Poseidon's body. Finally, we came to the end of the room, and the stairs were in sight. I stopped for a moment to look out of another small window.

"Uh-oh."

"What's wrong?"

"Euryale isn't at her post anymore," I said.

Janine climbed out of my pocket and leaned over the ledge. "Is that her walking toward the statue?" She pointed to a small figure moving slowly toward Poseidon. It looked like an ant.

"Probably. She doesn't seem to be in a hurry."

"I bet she thinks she'll just catch us when we come out of the big toe. She's too lazy to climb all these stairs." Janine harrumphed.

I hadn't thought of a way out of the statue. How could I be so stupid? Euryale didn't have to chase us. She'd just wait until we came out with the cheese and then eat us.

"Janine, this is a problem," I said. "How are we going to get past her on our way out? I already gave her all of my Port Salut."

"Robert!" Janine put her hands on her hips. "Do I have to think of everything?"

"I suppose." I couldn't help laughing. "What do you suggest?"

"Dad obviously didn't go out through the toe. We need to use the back door."

"Of course," I said, thinking there probably was no back door. "We'd better hurry up then. Come on." Janine hopped back into my pocket, and we turned to go.

I climbed up another seven flights before our stairway forked. One path continued up, probably into Poseidon's neck and head, and the other went down at an angle. I took the path that obviously was his arm. The stairs traveled straight downward for about fifty feet, no back and forth between flights. They smoothed out with a ninety-degree right turn and went on as a level path, ending in a semi-circular room.

I opened a door in one wall and found a spiral staircase going straight up. We must have been in Poseidon's hand. The staircase was the handle of his trident. It went down also. I stared into its dark, descending curve. It probably would have been a lot quicker to come up that way, but Euryale never told us about it. I shouldn't have been so quick to take her advice about getting in. She sent us the

124

long way on purpose. Dirty rat.

"Yoo-hoo." I heard a familiar voice echoing up the stairway. My pulse quickened.

"Don't worry now. I'll be up shortly." Euryale's voice gave me a headache. "I'm not as young as I used to be, you know," she complained.

"I bet she moves fast when she wants to," Janine whispered.

"Yeah, we'd better hurry." I started up the staircase two steps at a time. Dizzy from the stairs' constant turning, I had to keep my hands out against the walls so I didn't crash my head into the stone. It was narrow, stuffy, and exhausting.

At last, I reached what I could only guess was the bottom of the trident's spears. I emerged from the stairs into a small room with three vertical tubular passages overhead. There was no way to climb them, but dim light from each passage joined to illuminate one spot in the center of the floor.

"Robert, that's it," Janine said excitedly, "it's a trap door!" She was right. I reached down and pulled on a small brass handle that lay flush with the floor.

"Where *are* you, children?" Euryale's echo reached us. "I can't climb another step. I'll just wait for you here."

How could she have reached Poseidon's hand so quickly?

"I told you she's faster than she lets on," Janine chirped. "Hurry up, Robert."

The door opened and a small chamber, about two feet by four feet, came into view. My heart sank. The cheese wasn't there. "What do we do now?" I crumbled to the floor.

"You didn't expect the cheese to be there, did you?" Janine berated me.

"Well, yeah, I did."

"Come on, Robert. You know Dad must have the cheese if he made it this far. We just need to figure out how to get out of here."

"Let me see." I got irritated with Janine for the first time in several hours. "We're about half a mile in the air. Sharp-toothed snake-lady is waiting for us to come down the stairs, and I don't know how to fly. What do you want us to do?"

"For starters," Janine said, smirking, "why don't you read that note?"

I looked back into the chamber to see a folded piece of paper lying in one corner. I gave Janine the eye, snatched it up, and unfolded it.

"What's it say?" she peered over my thumb.

"It's just a bunch of letters, must be some kind of code."

"Let's get crackin' then," Janine said. Her enthusiasm never seemed to wane.

I stared at the puzzle. "It looks like a word find," I said.

"Yeah. I could have told you that." Janine snorted through her nose.

I dug a pencil out of my pack and started circling words I recognized. "Hey, they're all cheeses."

"Does that surprise you?" Janine asked.

"I guess it shouldn't." I continued circling. I had about eight cheeses circled when I ran out of words. "That can't be it," I moaned, "too many uncircled letters."

"Hey, don't you have a list of all those weird cheeses on you somewhere?" Janine asked.

"Janine, you're brilliant," I said.

"I know." She smiled.

There was another small book in my pack, entitled Cheese Directory. I pulled it out and quickly finished circling the other cheeses. When I finished the puzzle, this is what I found:

```
A M E R I C A N E B L U E N C A M E M B E R T E
C O L B Y M C R E A M Y E D A M H F E T A E F R
O M A G E R G O U D A E J A R L S B E R G S M A
R S C A P O N E H O R M O N T E R E Y J A C K T
C M O Z Z A R E L L A U N E U F C H A T E L T S
W I S S P R O V O L O N E T Q U E S O U B L A N
C O N R I C O T T A N S T R I N G E S W I S S L
```

"So what do we do with this?" she asked.

"Maybe the extra letters mean something?" I said, shrugging my shoulders.

I scribbled the unused letters down on the back of the directory. "Hey, I'm right. Look, Janine," I showed her. "If we use all the letters that don't make words, this is what it says, ENEMY HERE SHORTCUT TUNNEL."

"I don't see any tunnels." She scanned the little room.

"You don't think he means the skylights?" I asked, looking upward.

"You got any rope?" Janine looked up. The ceiling was about ten feet above our heads, and the walls were smooth.

"No."

"Children, I'm waiting." Nasty Euryale's voice floated through the doorway. "Don't make me come up and get you."

"Look at your puzzle again," Janine demanded. "You must have missed something."

I scanned the paper. The cheeses were listed in alphabetical order. "Janine, look. Swiss is circled twice, and one of them is out of order."

"So?" She stared blankly at me.

"Wait." I ran my finger along the letters. "The Swiss

128

that's out of order is right after the "t" for shortcut and before the "t" for tunnel. I think it should read, ENEMY HERE SHORTCUT SWISS TUNNEL."

"Great, Robert!" Janine cried, "I'll take a Swiss tunnel, an American tunnel, even a Greek tunnel. But I don't see any tunnels!"

"Don't panic, Janine. Let's check the field guide." For once, I'd thought of something before she did. I grabbed the book from my pack and flipped straight to the index. "Here it is: tunnels, page 198." Turning to page 198, I found the section on "Experimental Travel." I read aloud,

> *"Our research scientists have almost perfected a new wormhole method of locomotion. The passages through uncut Baby Swiss have proven to have exceptional transport power. By placing your index finger into one of the tunnel entranceways and speaking the name of your destination, you can be transported at light speed. We must caution that this method of travel is not yet stable and is not recommended unless the agent finds him or herself in a dire emergency."*

"That's it!" Euryale's irritated voice came through the doorway. Her dragging body followed a second later. Breathing heavily, she said, "You children have played hard to get." She leaned against the wall for a minute to catch her breath. I guess she was pretty old. Then she smacked her lips while all her snake hairs licked the air with their forked tongues. "I think I'll dine on you slowly." She looked up at me, and I saw the hunger in her eyes.

As I slammed the book shut, I felt Janine scamper down my back.

"Euryale!" I crooned, trying to buy some time until I could find the Baby Swiss in my pack. "So glad you could make it."

"I'll just bet you are." She smiled, snakes hissing. "I'm going to thoroughly enjoy you and your bratty little sister." She approached me with her teeth bared and her nails raised.

As I backed up against the wall, fumbling for my pack, I heard a squeaky voice shout "Marco Montasio."

The last thing I saw was the surprise on Euryale's twisted face as it vanished from my sight.

Chapter 13

Mazes and Manticores

The split second after Euryale's face disappeared from my view, I tumbled to a stop in the middle of a marshy swamp. Talk about needing to work on the Swiss tunnel mode of locomotion. Oozing, brown muck dripped from my hands, my shirt, and my pants. It leaked from everywhere. I stood up, checking for broken bones. It was a relief to know I wouldn't have to worry about that Gorgon anymore.

"Janine!" I called, opening my backpack to see if she was all right. She sat comfortably atop the hunk of Swiss cheese, nibbling a tiny piece she'd broken off from the corner.

"Pretty quick, don't you think?" she asked with her mouth full of cheese.

"Yeah. Good call on getting into the pack. Euryale would have eaten us for sure if you hadn't thought of finding the Swiss."

"Don't worry, Robert." Janine smiled sweetly. "I'll

always take care of you. Do you see Dad anywhere?"

I scanned the surroundings. Immense trees rose from the swampy floor. Their long skinny branches reached back down like fingers trying to grab me. Their giant bases curved in and out like snakes before disappearing into the black, still water. Hairy, green vines hung menacingly around my head while mosquitoes whined in my ear. Tiny islands of drier ground sprung up every few feet. My clothes clung to me because of the hot dampness. I didn't like the looks of the place.

"Yuck," Janine said after she'd climbed back onto my shoulder. "This place gives me the creeps, and it's almost as stinky as that cheese Mikrainos took. I don't see Dad, though."

"Remember, the book said the Swiss cheese wasn't stable yet. I bet he's around somewhere."

"Let's go, Robert. There's no telling what you're standing in."

"My sentiments exactly," I said. I lifted my foot, and with a great sucking sound, the mud released it. I continued trudging through the marsh muck until I reached the first spot of higher ground where I climbed up its slippery rise and stopped to rest on a decaying stump. Crawly black things scattered when I threw down my pack. Gross.

It was impossible to see any sort of landmark or even the sun from our position. I knew a little about navigating from my hiking trips with Dad, but I didn't have a compass or any point of reference from which to work. "Which way do you think we should go?"

"Too bad we don't have a map," Janine said as she climbed back down into my pocket and dangled her arms out of the front of it.

"Maybe we do." I dug back into the pack and took out one of Stefano's maps, the one that looked like Europe. I examined it more closely and saw it had many strange places labeled. "I wish I knew where we were."

"Why don't you ask the map?" Janine said, joking. "Maybe it will tell you."

"Janine, you're a genius!" I exclaimed.

"What?"

"Where are we?" I said to the map. Two small luminescent dots appeared on the map. "Awesome. It's like a GPS."

"What's a GPS?"

"It's a satellite system you can use to track where you are. Jimmy McCarty's dad has one in their car. It keeps him from getting lost."

"Cool," Janine said. "Maybe it can get us out of here."

"Uh-oh."

"What, uh-oh?" Janine said.

"That doesn't look good," I moaned.

"What doesn't look good?" She tried to look over the edge of the paper.

"See those two dots there? That's us. We're on the Island of the Lost."

"Oh. Maybe the map can lead us out." Janine was ever the optimist.

"Okay, I'll try." I looked dubiously at Janine. "How do we get out of here?" I said to the map. Nothing happened. I tried again. "Where is Marco Montasio?" Again, nothing. "Janine, I don't think this map can do anything but show us where we are."

"Maybe the old guidebook can shed some light the problem?" Janine asked.

"Right." I took out the guidebook and flipped again to the index. "Here it is, Island of the Lost, page 201."

"What's it say?"

I turned to page 201, to the chapter entitled "Places You Don't Want To Be" and gulped.

"Is it bad?" Janine looked at me.

I gazed down at her tiny face, realizing she was just a kid, and decided to leave out the worst of what I'd read.

"Not really. The swamp is like a giant maze. We're going to have to be very careful if we want to get out of here. We need some rope so we can mark our path and not travel around in circles."

"No problem," Janine said. "You've got a big ball of twine in your pack. I saw it when I went in after the Swiss cheese."

"Great," I said, forcing a smile. What page 201 really said was:

> *The Island of the Lost is the home of the fearsome manticore. Don't go there. If you do go, carry a good supply of Limburger. The only way off the island is by sea. Syndicate modes of transport are inoperable due to high humidity and a hostile atmosphere. Also, if you are unskilled in labyrinth work, remember to mark your way through the manticore's maze.*

Reaching into the backpack, I found the twine and took out a block of Limburger. I looked at it for a moment and broke off a small piece. I held it away from my nose because it was rank. "Here, Janine. Take it," I said, holding out the tiny corner to her.

"Gross! That stinks." Janine wrinkled her nose.

"Just take it."

"Hey, wait a minute." Janine looked accusingly at me. "Why do you want me to take that cheese? What's really wrong with this island?"

I knew she'd find out eventually. "Janine, the manticore lives here. It doesn't like the smell of Limburger cheese."

"Yeah, well. I don't like the smell of it either."

"Janine. This thing is dangerous. Really dangerous. But we ought to be okay as long as we have the Limburger with us. Please put it in your pockets for me." I had no idea how the Limburger would handle the manticore, but the fourth secret said, 'The manticore flees at the smell of Limburger cheese.' I hoped it would stay far away from us if it got a whiff of the Limburger.

"Oh, all right." Janine stuffed the cheese into her pockets. "Eww! Robert! It's getting all mashed up, and now it's all over my hands."

That gave me an idea. "Good, Janine. Spread it all over your jeans and your arms too."

"Robert, that is disgusting!"

"Do it!" I yelled at her. I started smearing Limburger all over my own arms and legs. Janine stared at me for a

136

moment longer, then did the same.

"Robert," she said, giggling, "we are the two smelliest people in the world."

"Yeah," I agreed, "Mikrainos would probably love us now. We'd better get going." I tied the end of the twine around the stump. I stepped back down into the muck and headed for the next muddy island. We traveled silently for about half an hour, in and out of stagnant water, around huge trees, and through choking vines. I tried to keep my path as straight as possible.

Abruptly, the swamp ended as I crested yet another island. The trees thinned and the ground became solid. Soon we reached an ancient, crumbling, wrought iron fence. It surrounded a mansion in about the same shape of disrepair.

"You think anybody lives there?" Janine whispered.

"It looks deserted," I murmured, afraid to break the stillness. I cut what was left of the twine, leaving our swamp path behind us, and crept along the perimeter of the fence. Soon we reached the back of the mansion. Here the thorny, overgrown remains of a formal garden surrounded a large hedge in the center. My eyes rested on the ten-foot high hedge. I knew immediately it was a labyrinth, a maze with high walls. Paths usually wind around in a labyrinth until they reach a center circle. There are many dead ends and ways to get lost inside. Dad's restaurant had one in the courtyard. People came from miles around to walk in it.

"NO!" Bellows and roars came from the direction of the labyrinth. "When will you cede, Montasio?" The voice cried out again, followed by more wails.

I looked at Janine in horror.

"Hurry, Robert," she said urgently. "That manticore thing has Dad."

Chapter 14

Into the Labyrinth

I dashed to the entrance of the labyrinth and was about to rush in when Janine said, "Wait!"

"Wait? What for? We've got to rescue Dad!"

"You know how we always got lost in the labyrinth at Dad's restaurant?" Janine reminded me.

"That would be you who always got lost," I corrected her. "I knew how to get in and out just like that."

"Right. After you practiced about a billion, gazillion times. You think this labyrinth has the same pattern as Dad's?" She looked at me.

I remembered how long it had taken me to solve the pattern in Dad's labyrinth. "Yeah, you're right. We'd better leave a trail so we can find our way out. Let me see what extra cheese I've got." I started rummaging through my backpack.

"Robert!" Janine yelled.

"What is it?"

She just stared at me.

"Or, maybe I'll use the twine," I said, smiling at her. "It's better than the cheese. What if there are mice or some other creatures around here who like cheese?"

"Oh, yeah. Good thinking, Robert," Janine said with a smirk.

"Well, I don't want to end up like Hansel and Gretel with the breadcrumb problem," I said again. At least this time Janine didn't have to tell me what to do.

"Let's do it," Janine said.

I tied the end of the string to a branch at the entrance of the labyrinth. I walked into the main opening and decided to turn right. As soon as we entered the labyrinth, the light dimmed. In Dad's labyrinth, if you turned right every time you had a choice, you ended up in the center. Then you had to turn left at every choice to get out.

I could not see over the walls, even when I stretched my neck. Because the hedges were thick, dark, and green, we couldn't see through them either. I started down the path and ran into a dead end almost immediately. Menacing laughter came from the walls around me.

"You have chosen incorrectly, Master Montasio," the condescending voice chided.

"Who said that?" I jumped and turned, half expecting to see the manticore behind me. No one was there.

"I am the spirit of the maze," the voice responded. "I see all that happens within my walls."

"Can you see our father?" Janine spoke up.

"Yes. He is in the center with that loathsome manticore."

"Will you guide us to the center?" I asked, my hopes rising.

"I cannot guide you," the voice said, laughing at us again. "I only observe and comment. You are not doing so well. You should turn around now."

"Right." I said. The maze spirit wasn't going to be much help. I rolled up the extra twine as I retraced my steps out of the dead end. When I reached the first intersection in the path, I looked at Janine. "Which one should we take?" It was a classic labyrinth intersection, with four choices, north, south, east, and west.

"That one will lead us back out." Janine pointed to the path that we had taken to enter the labyrinth. "We already tried the one we're on. So, that leaves us with the other two."

"We turned right for this path. Let's take the opposite one." I pointed to the lane directly ahead of us and started, trailing the string behind me again. I jogged along for a few minutes, thinking I'd found the correct path. It curved left and right. I decided to stay on it and not take any of the forks. As I rounded another corner, I ran smack into a leafy wall.

"Foiled again," the maze voice taunted me.

"If you aren't going to help us, I wish you'd shut up," Janine yelled at the invisible voice.

"Well, pardon me." The voice sounded insulted. "I think I will."

"Good riddance," Janine said.

I turned around and began rewinding the string when I heard the manticore again, "Answer the question, Montasio. Be quick, for I weary of toying with you." Silence ensued for a moment, then the manticore's frustrated screams rose again.

"He must not have liked what Dad said. Come on, Robert."

I rolled twine faster and ran back to our original intersection. There was only one more choice, so I quickly started down the last path. It curled and snaked for a very long time, finally coming to a triple junction.

"Which way do we go?" I looked at Janine for her advice.

"Take the middle one again, it worked last time." That was as good a choice as any, so I continued running down the path. The lane made a sharp right turn, and I stumbled out into the center of the labyrinth.

"Robert, look!" Janine pointed to the far side of the circular space. There my father stood, chained to a stone wall. His bruised and bloody body drooped. My heart leapt into my throat, and I couldn't answer Janine. I started to rush toward Dad when I spied the manticore, sitting with his back towards us. We needed a plan, so I backed up into the labyrinth for cover.

"Janine, hop up." I held my hand up for her to climb. As I raised her to my eye level, I could see her red, wet eyes. Shutting my own eyes to hold back the tears I said, "Janine, we've got to work together now to save Dad. I think I have a plan, but you'll have to be brave." When I opened my eyes, I saw her wiping her own snotty nose on her sleeve.

"I'm ready, Robert." She stood, proudly, as tall as her inch-high self would go.

"I think I've got to get the Limburger very close to the manticore, but someone has to bring Dad some of this Farmhouse Cheddar. It ought to help with all his bruises and cuts."

"That would be me?"

"Yeah, take as much as you can. You're going to have

to walk to Dad. If you don't make any noise the manticore probably won't see you."

"Okay, let's do it." Janine filled her pockets with as much Cheddar as possible, and broke off the biggest piece she could carry. It still wasn't very much, but it would have to be enough to get Dad back on his feet.

"I'll wait here for five minutes. Do you think that will give you enough time to walk across the yard?"

"Yeah, I'll be quick." Janine was about to depart when we heard the manticore again. We both peeked out from around the hedge.

"Okay, Montasio. Break time is over. Try this one on for size. Those we caught, we threw away. Those we could not catch, we kept. What were they?" He pranced around my father.

The picture in the book had not done him justice. His teeth, all stained brown and red, looked like jagged spear tips. His head must have been three feet across, with a shaggy mane sticking out wildly in every direction. There were so many poison darts ready to be launched from his tail that he could probably kill whomever he wanted instantly. He was huge, ugly, and evil-looking.

"Robert, why is he asking him that riddle?"

I tried to remember what the book said. Then, I

realized what was happening.

"Janine, manticores ask riddles of their prey before they kill them. Dad's probably been a prisoner here for a long time. As long as Dad keeps answering the riddles he'll be safe. Run now, while he's preoccupied with Dad."

Janine sped off as fast as her short little legs would go. "Make me proud, little sister," I whispered. It didn't take long for me to lose sight of her. That was good. I doubted the manticore would find her.

"Answer me now!" roared the manticore. He clutched Dad by the throat and glared at him. Dad mouthed something I couldn't hear.

"Ahh!" The manticore threw him back against the wall and paced. "You know too much, Montasio. Even Homer could not answer that riddle, and his death came because of it."

That's my dad, the riddle master. He always loved riddles. He used to come home every day with a new one for me. Dad could answer riddles forever. I wondered if it was part of his Syndicate training.

The manticore threw itself back to the ground and sulked. He was probably tired of coming up with new riddles for my dad. How long had Dad been his prisoner, anyway? I had no idea where Janine was, but I looked at my watch. Five minutes had passed, and it was time to get started. I took another smelly piece of Limburger from my pack and unwrapped it. I crept slowly toward the manticore. If I could get within free throw distance, it would be easy to toss the cheese his way.

At about twenty feet from the creature, I loosened my wrist and let the Limburger fly. It hit the manticore on the head and landed with a "thud" about two feet from it. That was a good shot. I waited for him to run, but he just stood there rubbing his head. The manticore flees at the smell of Limburger cheese. What went wrong?

The manticore stopped rubbing his bushy mane, turned and glared straight at me. I froze. He bounded to me in two steps and put a smothering paw on my chest, knocking me to the ground. He kept his paw there, holding me in place. I decided not to resist.

"What have we here?" His shaggy head smiled. Up close, his teeth were worse than Euryale's. "Why, it's another Montasio." He extended his claws, ever so slightly, while he spoke. I winced as they sunk into my flesh. I felt a trickle of warm blood oozing from the scratches.

"We know what to do with you," he said. The manticore tossed me up and caught me in his mouth. I closed my eyes, thinking this was the end, but he didn't bite down. I hung like the lizards my cat delivers to our doorstep while the manticore carried me over to Dad and dropped me in the dirt. I looked up into Dad's eyes. He tried to smile through his puffy, purple face.

"Look, Montasio. I have a companion for you. This would not be your son, would it? I can see the resemblance. You're both so ugly." He snickered as he threw me into a chain next to Dad, clamping the shackles. "Quickly, now, young Montasio. I am famished. What is round as a bucket, deep as a cup, yet the entire ocean cannot fill it up?"

I knew the answer to this. It was a kid's riddle. I should have remembered it. My mind went blank as I panicked. I had to think. It cannot be filled because it has holes. The answer came back to me, and I looked straight into the manticore's evil eyes.

"A sieve."

"Twas but an amateurish puzzle for you. Try this one. What walks on four legs at dawn, two legs at noon, and three legs in the twilight?" He leered at me. "Be quick now!"

That was easy. It was the first riddle my Dad taught me. It was the riddle of the Sphinx. The Sphinx supposedly ate anyone who couldn't answer it. I'd always thought that was an old legend, but after today, I realized that anything was possible. I smiled as I looked up at the manticore. "A man," I said proudly.

"Humbug! You shall not foil me much longer. The next will be much more difficult." He returned to his resting place.

I felt some confidence coming on since answering his two riddles. "Hey, manticore," I bravely called out. He looked up at me, growling.

"You shall kindly address me as Daimonas."

"Daimonas, I have a question for you."

"I generally do not answer questions from my captives, but your father has bored me for so long that I should like to entertain a change of pace." He motioned for me to continue.

"Why didn't you run when I hit you with that Limburger cheese?"

He looked around anxiously. Spying the Limburger, he kicked it away. "Sorry, old chap. I have a terrible head cold. I can't smell a thing." He leered at me as he cleaned his beard with his paws.

I turned my attention to Dad. Janine was climbing up his arms. When she reached his shoulder, she whispered into his ear. He struggled to turn his head toward her. She popped a bit of Cheddar into his mouth. He did not have the strength to chew it, so he sucked on it until it melted on his tongue. Janine continued to feed him the Cheddar until her supply was gone. He seemed a little stronger, but not much.

"Janine," I whispered, trying to avoid capturing the manticore's attention. "Come get some more Cheddar out of my pack." Understanding, Janine climbed down Dad's back and up mine. A few minutes later, I saw her feeding him some more cheese. Now he managed to stand up without hanging his head.

"Robert," he croaked. "It's good to see you."

Chapter 15

Janine Saves the Day

The manticore approached, and I whispered to Dad, "Droop your head again. Don't let Daimonas see that you're stronger." Dad obliged, and Daimonas danced around me, his new quarry.

"Young Montasio, here is your next riddle. What is the only thing you can keep by giving it away?"

I racked my brain, trying to pull something out of my memory. Daimonas grew impatient, snarling and swishing his pointy barbed tail. I looked at Dad.

"No help from your elders." Daimonas shook his head at me.

Give it? Keep it? What could I give and keep at the same time? Staring into the dirt, I saw Dad's foot tracing out letters, W—O—R.

"Enough! You are out of time. I will have your answer now, young Montasio. I am hungry."

"What can you keep by giving it away?" I smiled at Daimonas. "Your word." If you give someone your word,

150

that's the only way to keep it, like keeping a promise.

Daimonas huffed back across the courtyard and slumped down again. He gave a giant yawn, got up, and walked around in a circle before plopping down and closing his eyes. In a minute, he was snoring loudly. This gave me some time to think.

"Dad," I whispered. "How are we going to get away? Daimonas can't smell the Limburger."

"I can smell it though. What did you two do, bathe in it?"

"Not exactly." Janine giggled. "We rubbed it all over ourselves."

"Smart children," Dad whispered.

"Somehow we need to get it into his nose," I said.

"Yuck!" Janine squealed.

The thought grossed me out, but I knew there was only one thing to do. "Janine, it's up to you to get us out of this mess."

"I know," she said. "You two are kind of tied up." She laughed at her own joke. "What do I have to do?"

"You're going to have to climb up Daimonas' back, down his forehead and stick the Limburger up his nose." I grinned because, for once, she'd have to do the dirty work. "He'll be able to smell it from that close," I said.

"Eww. Gross!" She looked at our dad.

"You're our only hope, Janine," he said.

"Okay, I'll do it." She scampered into my pack to collect some more Limburger.

"Janine," I said softly when she climbed back onto my shoulder, "I'm proud of you. Good luck."

She smiled and said, "You owe me one, a big one."

I watched her sneak across the yard to where the manticore lay. He continued to snooze, probably dreaming of having me for breakfast. I guess coming up with riddles for us was hard work. As she climbed up his furry back, I lost sight of her for a minute, but she emerged on the top of his head, waving to us.

She climbed quickly down his nose, shoved two fistfuls of Limburger into Daimonas' nostrils, and started climbing back to the top of his head as fast as possible.

Daimonas awoke with a start and looked to the left and right but could find no one. He began shaking his head madly. Janine had reached the spot between his ears. She hung on to the ends of his fur, flailing like an old dust rag.

Suddenly, after another violent shake of Daimonas' head, she let go and sailed through the air. She landed neatly on a grassy spot just to our left. The grass must have cushioned her fall because she popped right up and ran toward us.

The manticore roared and screamed, pawing his nose. I guess that Limburger really stung. He ran around in circles and whined. After another minute, Daimonas sprang over the hedge of the labyrinth, screaming, "I will have my revenge, Montasio." His moans continued in the distance for another minute, then all was quiet.

"I did it!" Janine squealed as she reached us.

"Well done, Janine," Dad whispered. "Now, can you find a tube of cheese spread in Robert's pack?"

"Dad, you hate cheese spread." I looked at him, remembering how he always told me it was not fit to eat.

"I don't like to eat it, but it's great for dissolving the metal on our handcuffs." Another piece of useful information I would have to keep stored away.

Janine came back up to my shoulder licking the slimy cheese spread. "This is great stuff. Robert, you want some?" She held out her hand to me.

"No, Janine, rub it onto my handcuffs."

"Okay." She reached up and put some onto the metal hinge. It smoked and sizzled before cracking. I was free. I got some more out of my pack and put it on Dad's chains. He fell forward onto his knees, still weak.

"Here Dad," I said, grabbing some more Cheddar, "eat some more of this." He took the cheese and nibbled some slowly. Then he sat up and opened his arms.

"Robert, Janine. I've thought about you every day since Daimonas caught me."

I hugged him tightly, blinking back my tears.

"Dad, what about me?" Janine said. "Do you have that mystic cheese? I'm about ready to get unshrunk."

"Janine, how'd you get to be so small anyway?" Dad looked at her through misty eyes.

"Well." She looked down. "Madame G. says it was Robert's fault, but the truth is, I grabbed her elixir out of his hand and drank it."

I sat there, dumbfounded. This was a first—Janine taking responsibility for her own actions.

"You'll have to tell me the whole story later. But now, I happen to have, here in my coat pocket," Dad said as he reached into his field jacket, "the mystical cheese of Eliki, which has cost me two years in this forsaken place with Daimonas." He pulled out a blue-skinned wheel of dried up, old cheese.

"It doesn't look that impressive," I said.

"Looks can be deceiving, Robert. Let's see if it is as powerful as we think." He broke off the tiniest piece and held it out for Janine. She reached over, took the crumb of cheese, and sat back on my shoulder, munching it.

"It tastes moldy," she said.

"Remember, it's over three thousand years old," Dad began. As he spoke, Janine shrieked and in a poof of blue smoke regained her former size.

"Hey, get off of me," I yelped as I fell to the ground under her weight. Janine sat sprawled across my chest.

"I'm me! I'm me!" Janine ran around in a circle dancing. "Look, I'm me again!"

"Janine, you were always you. You're just not a miniature version anymore," I said. We all laughed. "Dad, shouldn't we head out of here before Daimonas comes back?"

"You don't have to worry about him. It'll be a month before he recovers from that Limburger Janine stuck up his nose."

"Don't remind me," Janine said, twisting up her own nose.

"Nevertheless, we had better be on our way. I do miss your mother. We cannot use Syndicate transport here, so we need to head to the beach. Triton's fellows will give us a lift."

"You mean Delfini?" I asked.

"You've met Delfini?"

"Yes. It was my favorite part of the trip."

"Let's go then. It may take some time to find our way out of here."

"Not to worry, Dad," Janine said, "I remembered to mark our path. Our string is waiting at that entrance over there." She pointed across the yard to where we came into the center of the labyrinth.

"Smart girl," Dad said, putting his arm around her shoulder.

"Dad, we are Montasios, after all," Janine said.

We found the end of the twine, and I rolled it up as we retraced our steps. After we exited the labyrinth, Dad brought us around the front of the house, which faced a wide tree-lined path. We followed the path about a half a mile to the seashore. There, Dad pulled a conch from his pocket (I suppose I should have hung on to mine) and whistled. Our dolphin friends appeared. I was pleased to see Delfini in the group. She carried me, while Dad and Janine each got their own dolphins to ride.

"Ah, young Robert," Delfini said as we swished through the ocean, "I had great confidence in you. I see that all has ended well."

I was so happy I could not speak. Dad was there. I

was riding a dolphin, and soon we would be home with Mom.

As we said good-bye to the dolphins on the mainland coast, I felt just the slightest twinge of sadness that my journey was ending. I guessed that tomorrow I would be back in school, like every other normal thirteen-year-old.

We walked along the beach idly for a while. "Dad, does Mom know about your work with the Syndicate?"

"Yes, she does."

"Why didn't she tell us about it when you disappeared? I thought all this time that you had deserted the family." The pain of that memory still burned a bit.

"I'm sorry, Robert. And I apologize to you too, Janine. I had to keep my activities secret. Your mother is not a Montasio by birth. Therefore, she cannot participate in the Syndicate. She knows that, when you come of age, each of you will be given the opportunity to join. However, she made me promise not to reveal any Syndicate business to you until you were old enough to make an informed choice about whether to take on the dangerous tasks it involved."

"Then why did Madame G's elixir come to me? I'm only thirteen."

"Fifteen is considered the age of reason in the Syndicate.

I'd bet after they couldn't find me for such a long period of time, the Syndicate elders took a chance by bringing you in a little early. Only you could have completed my mission. The Syndicate is strictly a family business."

"Wow."

"And I came along as a bonus!" Janine smiled at me.

"I'm glad you were with me, sister." I rubbed her head.

"Let's get back to headquarters," Dad said.

"Okay, we need to look for a drunken goat," I said, scanning the horizon.

Dad fell into the sand, laughing. I did not see what was so funny.

"Robert, the drunken goat is not a goat. It's a cheese."

"What?"

"Didn't Stefano tell you that?"

"Stefano told me very little. He was in such a big rush to get me out of there."

"It was a big risk, but Stefano probably suspected that Daimonas had me and I wasn't going to last forever. Well, I hope you have some in your pack because I used mine on the Island of the Lost, but it didn't work."

"Dad, I've looked in all my compartments. I never saw

a cheese called 'Drunken Goat of Spain.'"

"Yes, but did you see one named 'Cabra borracha?'"

"Let me see." I dumped my pack. A small wheel of purple-skinned cheese tumbled out.

"That's it," Dad said. He grabbed it and sliced everyone a small piece. We each ate it, and the beach faded slowly to black.

The light reappeared like a dawning sun, and I realized a crowd of people surrounded us. Whispers and shouts of congratulation filled my ears. It took another moment before I recognized faces. There was Madame Gorgonzola and Stefano. We were in the Syndicate headquarters.

"Friends of cheese," Madame G. spoke up and the chatterings fell silent. "We greet today our long lost brother, Marco Montasio." She gestured toward my dad and applause broke out. He bowed graciously.

"Members of the Syndicate," Dad spoke up, "I have returned from my quest and bring you that which we sought—The Mystic Cheese of Eliki." He removed the cheese from his pocket with great flourish. Everyone went wild. "I present it to our beneficent leader in the hope that we may discover how to use it to restore peace, harmony, and good taste to our world."

"Friends," Madame G. spoke again and everyone

hushed. "Our gratitude goes to Marco, and to his son, Robert, without whom he may have been lost to us forever." Murmurs of assent swept through the crowd. "And now, the time to decide has come. Shall we give Robert Montasio full membership into our Syndicate? All in favor say 'Aye.'"

A chorus of enthusiastic "Ayes" went up. I was stunned. They wanted me as an agent? This was great!

"What about me?" Janine stepped up. "I helped too, you know."

"Ah, yes, Janine, dear." Madame G. turned to address her. "I see that you have really grown during this adventure, no?"

"Yes!" Janine put her hands on her hips.

"Then you will understand that you are not yet old enough to become an Agent of Cheese, no?"

Janine thought about it for a minute. "I guess so," she said, shuffling her feet. "But can I assist Robert on some of his missions?" she asked. "He's helpless without me."

"Perhaps that can be arranged, Janine, perhaps." Madame Gorgonzola touched her lightly on the head. "And now, it is time for you to return to Mrs. Montasio. Farewell, friends. Until we meet again."

With that, we whisked out of headquarters, through

the green cyclonic rush of wind I had first experienced when I came to meet Madame G. The bottle spit us out into my bedroom.

"Robert, I can see you haven't gotten any neater in my absence," Dad said.

"Sorry, Dad."

"Keep your bottle in a safe place. It's your portal into headquarters."

"You think I'll really get to go on another mission?"

"I'd bet on it." He smiled and gave Janine a hug.

"Come on. Let's go find your Mom."

Acknowledgments

I want to thank the many people who helped me create this book. First, to my wonderful editor, Madeline Smoot, who guided me through the grueling process from acceptance to publication. Who knew there were so many details to consider? Second, to the rest of the Blooming Tree and CBAY staff who gave the story its first chance: Miriam Hees and Kay Pluta, specifically. Third, to my beautiful and crazy critique group, the BQ's: Jacqueline, Natisha, Rose, Samantha, and Sandy. You girls rock! Fourth, to my precious children, Stephen, Aimee and Joseph, for their inspiration and expert reader opinions. Fifth, to my excellent husband, Steve, for his support and sage advice. Sixth, to my high school English teacher, Patricia Melancon, for telling me I could. And last, but not least, to God, for such an abundant life.

About the Author

Donna St. Cyr enjoys life in Baton Rouge, Louisiana, where she has worked as a teacher and school librarian for over twenty years. *The Secrets of the Cheese Syndicate* is her first book.

Visit Donna on her website at www.donnastcyr.com for additional information on her book, school visits, and more.